SOI

Solitaire, her kindly Uncle Jim's house in the Vendée region of France, represented a welcoming haven after years of unhappiness—but Marty arrived there to find her uncle gone and in his place a hard, unwelcoming stranger—Luc Dumarais. There would be no haven at Solitaire now, she realised. And if she did not get away quickly, there would be even more unhappiness . . . for Luc Dumarais was right out of her league . . .

SOLITAIRE

BY

SARA CRAVEN

MILLS & BOON LIMITED
17–19 FOLEY STREET
LONDON W1A 1DR

First published 1979
Australian copyright 1979
Philippine copyright 1979
This edition 1979

© Sara Craven 1979

ISBN 0 263 73104 9

Set in Linotype Plantin 10 on 11pt.

Made and printed in Great Britain by
Richard Clay (The Chaucer Press), Ltd, Bungay, Suffolk

CHAPTER ONE

As she got down from the small country bus, the heat seemed to strike her like a blow. A glance at her watch told Marty Langton that it was already past noon, and that, of course, explained why the small square seemed almost deserted. She had been in France for less than a week, but already she had become accustomed to the way everything seemed to grind to a complete halt at lunchtime so that the French could give *le déjeuner* their full and serious attention.

She put her case down at her feet, flexing her shoulder muscles wearily. In spite of the breeze from the open window she had managed to station herself beside, it had been a long hot journey, but now it was over at last. She had finally arrived in Les Sables des Pins.

Behind her the bus, having discharged the remainder of its passengers, started on its way again with a roar and a whiff of exhaust fumes. As it passed Marty, the driver leaned out of his seat and called something to her. She didn't catch the words—at school she'd always been considered good at French, but her experiences so far had soon disabused her of that notion; no one had told her about regional accents or that people spoke so *fast*—but the tone was friendly and encouraging as if he had discerned there was something a little forlorn about the slender figure standing looking round the square, with all her worldly goods packed into the elderly leather suitcase at her feet. She smiled rather shyly and lifted a hand in response as the battered vehicle clattered and swayed over the cobbles and around the corner out of sight.

When it had finally disappeared altogether, and even the raucous note of its engine was becoming a memory, Marty felt a faint quiver of apprehension run through her. She had been lonely before many times during her short life, but she had never felt so completely alone as she did at that moment. And all she had to sustain her was the promise of Uncle Jim's letter, reposing safely in her handbag.

'You're not alone,' she told herself fiercely and silently. 'Uncle Jim is waiting for you as he said he would be all those years ago. There's nothing to worry about. You're going to have a proper home at last.'

A proper home! Even though she had actually arrived, she could still hardly believe it. Only a month ago she had been working at her secure boring job in a solicitor's office, going home in the evenings to help Aunt Mary with the housework and the gardening at the big rather ugly Edwardian villa on the edge of the small town where they lived, and listen to her accounts of the day's events in the faintly complaining tone she habitually used. Aunt Mary had always had a grudge against the world in general, but this had been intensified fourteen years earlier when she had been forced to offer a home to her small orphaned niece. This had been a burden and an encumbrance she had never desired, and she had made Marty, five years old and shocked to the core of her being by the sudden death of her mother from virus pneumonia, fully aware of the fact.

All her young life she'd heard the recital of the various grievances—the difficulties of supporting a growing girl on a fixed income, the wish to travel, thwarted by Marty's presence—and it was only as she grew older that Marty began to realise that she was the excuse and not the cause for the shortcomings in her aunt's life. That Miss Barton was an indolent woman who preferred grumbling to exerting herself in any way. But by then it was too late. The idea that she was a nuisance and a burden to her aunt was firmly fixed in Marty's mind, and there could never be any real affection between them.

That was why Uncle Jim had come to assume such importance to her, she supposed. He had made the fact of his caring, his anxiety for her so clear from the outset. He wasn't in the strict sense of the word an uncle at all, of course, but a distant and much older cousin of her late father's, and many of Marty's earliest memories were connected with him. There was never any pattern to Uncle Jim's visits—he just arrived, and there were always presents when he did come, and a lot of laughter.

Marty smiled a little as she picked up her case and started determinedly across the square. Even her mother, whose eyes had never really lost their sadness after her young husband had been killed in a works accident, laughed when Uncle Jim came. Only Aunt Mary had disapproved, her openly voiced opinion that her young sister had married beneath her never more evident than when Uncle Jim was in the vicinity.

'Really, Tina,' Marty had overheard her say impatiently, 'I can't imagine why you encourage that man to come here. There's bound to be talk whether he was a relation of Frank's or not. And he's a most unsuitable influence to have on an impressionable child. Why, he's little better than a nomad. He's never had a settled job or a respectable home in his life.'

She could not hear her mother's soft-voiced reply, but Marty heard Aunt Mary's scandalised snort in response.

'You can't be serious, Tina! Isn't one mistake enough for you? A man like that—and he must be at least twenty years older than you. Have some sense before it's too late!'

Years later, Marty could still remember her mother's laugh, warm and almost carefree, with another underlying note that she was too young to understand then. Yet only a few weeks later, a neighbour had come to fetch her from school, telling her soothingly that her mummy didn't feel too grand, and before twenty-four hours had passed Tina Langton had died in hospital.

Marty's eyes misted suddenly as she sank down on one of the wrought iron chairs set outside the café under a striped awning. Uncle Jim had been off on his travels again, so there had been no way to tell him her mother had died—not that Aunt Mary would probably have done so even if there had been a forwarding address, she thought. So he had missed the funeral, and she had travelled south with Aunt Mary, thin-lipped and brooding beside her at this unexpected turn in her affairs.

At first the bewildered child she had been had thought she would never see Uncle Jim again, but she had been wrong, because he had turned up about six months later—'like the proverbial bad penny', Aunt Mary had remarked caustically, but she had not prevented Marty from seeing him, either then or on the few subsequent visits, and Marty supposed she should be grateful to her for that.

She had been nine the last time he came, she remembered, and breaking her heart because she had been asked to take part in a play at school and Aunt Mary had refused point blank to make her the necessary costume. He had noticed her red eyes and subdued manner at once and taken her on to his knee while Aunt Mary, rigid with resentment, had gone to the kitchen to make the pot of tea she considered sufficient to fulfil the laws of hospitality.

'What is it, lass?' He had smoothed her thick bob of chestnut hair with a massive but infinitely gentle hand. 'Aren't you happy here? It's a grand house, and I'm sure your aunt does her best for you.'

'I don't want her best.' Marty had wound her arms round his neck. 'I want you, Uncle Jim.'

He was very silent for a long time, then he said quietly, 'So be it, Tina. I can't take you with me now, because I don't know where I'm bound for and that's no life for a child. But one day, my chick, I'll find a place to settle down in and then I'll send for you—just as I'd meant ...' He'd stopped then, but Marty had known with an odd instinct that he'd been going to say, 'just as I'd meant to send for your mother', and she thought rather sadly that maybe if he'd just taken her with him four years earlier, her mother might still be alive and happy. And it didn't matter that he'd called her Tina either, because she knew that in some strange way in Uncle Jim's eyes, she and her mother were the same person.

He'd gone then, after drinking his tea and wishing Miss Barton 'Good afternoon' with more civility than sincerity, and Marty had not seen him again. Occasionally there had been a letter, and even more rarely a parcel, but none of them ever contained the hoped-for summons, and after a while the demands of school had begun to blur his image in her mind, and when she thought of him at all it was in the terms of a childhood fantasy.

A young woman emerged from the café to take her order and Marty asked her for an Orangina. Her throat was parched from the dust and heat of travelling. She was hungry too, and when she glanced through the beaded curtain that hung over the open doorway she saw that the adjoining room to the bar was a restaurant, and that there were menus posted on a small board at the side. She felt in her handbag for her wallet and counted her remaining francs. She had enough for a meal, if it wasn't too expensive, and then she would set about finding her way to Uncle Jim's house. Les Sables des Pins didn't look a very big town, and she was sure she would have little difficulty in finding her way to Solitaire, as he'd told her it was called.

She got out his creased and much folded letter and read it again. It was not the letter of a man who had ever had much to do with words, but it was hardly the illiterate scrawl that Aunt Mary had derisively dismissed it as.

It had not been a long letter either, but it told Marty all that was necessary.

'After all these years,' he'd written. 'I've finally found a place I can call home, and it's yours too, Tina, if you still want it. I've no relative other than you in the world, so everything I have—the flower farm and the house—will be yours when I've gone. It's very beautiful here in the spring, Tina, when the bulbs have bloomed, and each year in April there's a flower festival in Les Sables des Pins. That's

the nearest town, and it's just as it sounds with acres of
pine forests running down to the longest beach you've ever
seen. My house is by itself in the forest—I suppose that's
why the chap that built it called it Solitaire. A bit of a fancy
name, but I like it, and I hope that you will too.'

He had enclosed a small coloured snapshot of the house,
and as Marty studied it she felt her spirits rise perceptibly.
Who couldn't be cheered by the prospect of going to live in
a long, low house, its red-tiled roof, and dark green shutters
providing a dramatic contrast to the stark white of the
exterior?

There was a man standing near the front door and at first
glance she had assumed it was Uncle Jim, but when she
looked more closely she saw that he was a much younger
man, taller than Uncle Jim, and with dark almost black hair
where Jim's was fair turning to grey. Or had been when she
saw him last. He was probably completely grey by now.

She'd looked through the letter, stirred by a vague in-
explicable curiosity about the man in the photograph, but
there had been no clue to his identity.

Marty drank her Orangina gratefully when it came, and
then bestirred herself to look at the menu. As usual there
was a choice of meals at various prices, and after some wist-
ful lingering over the menus that offered grilled shrimps
and *moules marinières* as starters, she decided to settle for
the *plat du jour*—a thick slice of rare roast beef, accompanied by a steaming dish of *pommes frites*, and preceded
by a delicious home-made *terrine* with a side-dish of tomato
salad in an aromatic dressing.

In spite of some inner qualms of nervousness at the prospect of meeting Uncle Jim again after all these years her
healthy young appetite would not be denied, and she sat
back at last with a sigh of repletion, blinking her eyes
sleepily in the sun as she drank her coffee and toyed with
one of the nectarines that had been served as a dessert.

If the worst came to the worst, she told herself, and
Uncle Jim had not received her letter in reply, telling him

that she was on her way, or even if he was away, she had
enough money to supply her with a night's lodging here in
Les Sables, or even two nights if it came to the pinch.
There had been a generous amount of francs enclosed in
Uncle Jim's letter, and she had converted her own small
savings into travellers cheques as well.

It was probably this more than anything, she thought,
that had convinced Aunt Mary that she was really going to
France.

'You've closed your savings account?' Her aunt had
stared at her as if she had gone mad. 'What on earth has
possessed you, child? You surely haven't been taken in by
the boasts of that ridiculous old vagabond? You've no idea
what kind of conditions he may be living in. He probably
wants an unpaid housekeeper to look after him. A French-
woman would drive too hard a bargain for him, so he's
thought of you, after all these years without a word.'

Marty bit her lip, willing herself to be silent, while she
flinched at the scathing nature of her aunt's remarks. She
had always known that Aunt Mary would not be pleased to
hear of her plans, but she had not expected quite such a
vitriolic reaction. And she could have replied hotly that she
was little more than an unpaid housekeeper living where
she was, Aunt Mary having dispensed with the daily woman
she had employed for some years on economic grounds,
leaving the bulk of the heavy work to Marty at weekends.

Aunt Mary was going on. 'You'll make the biggest mistake of your life, my child, if you throw up everything
here. Your mother did exactly the same thing, and look
what a disaster that was—marrying a man of that class,
and then being widowed, left with a young child to bring
up. I would have thought the example of her folly would
have taught you a thing or two.'

'And so it has,' Marty said hotly, unable to restrain her
anger any more at this slur on her mother. 'It taught me
that it's love that matters in this world, and even you can't
deny that my mother and father were happy together. And

Uncle Jim loves me, so even if this house in France is—a slum, I don't care.'

'I think you will.' Aunt Mary's lips were so tightly compressed that they had almost vanished. 'You are used to certain standards, my dear—standards that your father's family, good people though they may be, probably don't even know exist. And what kind of a life has Jim Langton been leading all these years? Heaven only knows, but it's doubtful whether he's ever been fit company for a young girl, especially someone with your upbringing. And you seriously intend to throw it all up and go to live in a country —where it's not even safe to drink out of the taps,' she added on a note of pure bathos.

Angry as she was, Marty could not help seeing the funny side of it all and a reluctant smile started to spread, but Aunt Mary had no sense of humour, and she reached forward and to Marty's shock slapped her hard across her face.

'This is no laughing matter,' she rapped, her own face alarmingly red. 'Understand this, if you leave here, if you go to that no-good tramp of a man, then I shall alter my will. Not a penny will you get, nor this house. And don't imagine that Jim Langton will cushion you against the hard times. Money flows through his hands like water. He's been totally improvident all his life, and it's unlikely that age has changed him.'

Marty stood very straight, her large grey eyes fixed on her aunt's furious face, the fingermarks standing out angrily on the pallor of her cheek.

'It isn't your money I want, Aunt Mary,' she said quite gently. 'It was always something that you couldn't give me —or weren't prepared to. Your love and your time. But there'll be plenty of that where Uncle Jim is. I shall always be grateful for what you've done for me,' she added, 'but I really don't want any more. You must do as you wish with your possessions. They're really none of my business.'

There was a long and fulminating silence and then Aunt Mary turned precipitately and left the room.

The following week, up to the time that Marty left to board the Hovercraft at Ramsgate for the Channel crossing, was not an easy time, full of strained silences and edged and embittered remarks. Miss Barton made no attempt to come and see Marty off, and Marty herself did not suggest it. She had been hurt by her aunt's assumption that she could be bought, and felt that any move towards a conventional leavetaking would be nothing short of hypocrisy. Her one tentative suggestion that she should write when she got to France and let her aunt know that she had arrived safely and that all was well was met with an icy 'It won't be necessary.' And when the front door of The Poplars finally closed behind her, Marty knew that an era in her life had come irrevocably to its end.

She could not drive, but even if she had possessed a licence she felt she would have thought twice about driving in France. Even before she got out of Calais, she saw some near-accidents involving tourists who had not got the hang of the French priority from the right. Her own journey was to be rather more sedate, on public transport, so that she could see something of the countryside on her way to the Vendée region of France where Les Sables des Pins was situated.

It wasn't a part of France that Marty really knew very much about, and her researches at the local library prior to her departure had not been very revealing, although she had discovered that La Rochelle was the nearest big town to Les Sables, and she knew that La Rochelle had played a major part in the tragic religious wars in France during the sixteenth and seventeenth centuries.

Her journey down to Les Sables might not have been a totally straightforward one, but she felt she could have had no better introduction to France. The trip through Anjou had been particularly enjoyable, and she had stayed overnight in Angers, taking time off to visit the chateau with its odd decapitated turrets—another relic of the religious wars. She was fascinated by the acres of vineyards stretching away on both sides of the road, and the little stalls set up at intervals urging passers-by to stop and taste some of the famous wines of Anjou. Marty would have loved to have done so, but the bus she was travelling on never seemed to stop at a convenient place, and she had to promise herself that she would get Uncle Jim to bring her one day.

She paid the bill for her meal, and asked Madame rather haltingly if she knew the whereabouts of a house called Solitaire. Madame's eyebrows rose a little, but her reply was immediate. But of course she knew of it. Who did not? Gladly she would direct Mademoiselle, but what did Mademoiselle seek there?

Marty hesitated, but only for a moment. After all, she told herself, there was no harm in telling this woman what the situation was.

'I'm going there to see the owner. He's my uncle,' she said, and smiled.

Madame's eyebrows ascended almost into her hairline, and Marty found herself hoping devoutly that all Aunt Mary's predictions about Uncle Jim's probable life-style were totally unfounded.

'*Est-ce possible?*' Madame asked the world in general, and went back into the café shaking her head. A moment later Marty saw her talking excitedly to a man behind the bar, and saw necks being craned in her direction. She felt hot with embarrassment and stood up decisively to take her leave. Obviously in spite of its placid appearance, Les Sables des Pins was a hotbed of gossip, she thought, and she had just supplied the main item for the day.

She was just about to leave when the man from behind the bar emerged and stood looking at her, frowning a little. He said, 'Mademoiselle desires to be directed to the Villa Solitaire, it is so?'

'Yes, please.' Marty set her case down rather resignedly.

He hesitated. 'Is Mademoiselle sure that she has the correct destination?'

'Quite sure.' Marty did not want to be rude, but some of

her weariness crept into her tone. 'Please tell me where it is. I've been travelling for most of the week, and I'm very tired. The journey took longer than I originally expected and my uncle will be worried if I don't arrive.'

His shrug seemed to be almost fatalistic. 'Then there is nothing more to be said.'

He might have seemed reluctant to vouchsafe them, but his directions were clear and concise and he even drew her a little map. Watching her tuck it away safely in the pocket of her shoulder bag, he asked 'Mademoiselle has a car? It is a fair distance.'

'No, but I'm sure I can manage.' Marty repressed a sigh as she looked up at the unclouded blue of the sky and felt the heat of the sun blazing down.

'That will not be necessary. Jean-Paul!' He gestured to someone sitting inside the café. He turned to Marty. 'He will take you,' he said rather abruptly.

'Oh, no, really!' Marty was appalled. 'I don't want to cause anyone any trouble.'

He shrugged again. 'What trouble?' he demanded. 'Each day he passes the Villa on his way to the beach.'

When Jean-Paul finally emerged, he turned out to be not a great deal older than Marty herself, but, she suspected as he looked her over with lingering appreciation, a great deal more versed in the ways of the world. He seized her case and carried it over to a small and battered Citroën parked in the shade of the church which dominated the square.

'You are English,' he said with an air of amazed discovery as he climbed into the front seat beside her and started the engine. 'Not many English come here to Les Sables. They prefer to visit Brittany, which is my own region where I was born.'

'Then why are you here?' Marty was glad to be asking the questions, determined to switch the focus of attention.

He was not in the least unwilling to reply. He was a student, she learned, working in the local *boulangerie* for the vacation, and he was fortunate that his shift worked at night so that he had the day for swimming and sunning himself. Judging by the deep tan he had already acquired, this must be how he spent the major part of each day, she surmised. She was just about to ask him about his studies, when he got in ahead of her with a question of his own.

'And yourself? You have come here to lie in the sun?'

'Perhaps,' she allowed. 'Actually I'm joining my uncle.' She paused. 'He owns the Villa Solitaire.'

Obviously startled, Jean Paul missed his gear change and swore under his breath.

'Your uncle?' he demanded. 'But no one has heard of any niece from England.'

'All the same he has written to me and asked me to join him,' she said coolly.

'*Mon dieu,*' he murmured, a smile playing about his lips. 'And how will Bernard respond to this, I ask myself?'

'Bernard?' Marty raised her brows interrogatively.

He slanted her an odd look. 'Your cousin, *ma petite*. The only son of your uncle. Is it possible you did not know of his existence, *hein*?'

'No, I didn't,' Marty managed after a pause. 'I—I didn't even know my uncle had married.'

'Well,' he gave a slightly cynical shrug as he accelerated past an elderly cyclist, 'I imagine he would not have been too eager to pass on the news. The marriage, from what I can gather, was not a success and they lived apart after the child was born. Bernard came to live with his father on the death of his mother just over a year ago.'

'Oh.' Marty digested this with a pang. She could not understand why Uncle Jim had given her no inkling of this in his letter. She could appreciate that he might be reluctant to admit that his venture into matrimony had been a failure, but surely the existence of a child made some mention of it obligatory. She wondered how old Bernard was, but was reluctant to ask Jean-Paul. Certainly Uncle Jim had left it late in life to marry. At her reckoning he must be at least in his late fifties by now, and she had always thought of him as the eternal bachelor, which was silly in a way as she was sure he had been in love with her mother and would have married her eventually.

She realised unhappily that she was feeling jealous and scolded herself for her selfishness. Just because she had always had this idea that Uncle Jim and she would be on their own, she had not bargained for a third party, especially one who could claim a closer relationship than she could.

And there was another strange thing. She was sure Uncle Jim's letter had said she was his only relative. Had the failure of his marriage embittered him against his son, so that he refused to acknowledge the relationship? With a sinking heart, it occurred to her that the haven she had envisaged might in fact contain stormier waters than she had ever encountered before.

They were out of the town by now, and driving along a narrow rather twisting road flanked by small neat houses whose pristine paintwork gleamed in the sun. There seemed to be sand everywhere—banked at the side of the road, and covering what earth there was in the gardens which seemed to be assiduously cultivated in spite of this. She could see a number of women, some of them wearing attractive sun-bonnets, working with hoes between neat rows of plants.

Beyond the houses she could see the deep brooding green of the pine forests, and it was not long before the houses became more scattered and gave way to the trees.

Jean-Paul glanced sideways at her rapt face and grinned. 'It would have been a long, hot walk for you,' he commented, and she was forced to agree. On each side of the narrow road, the banks rose steeply, the grass giving way to what seemed to be gorse bushes. Beyond this rose the trunks of the pine trees, dark and mysterious. But even here in the forest there were signs of habitation. Plots of land had been cleared and smart white houses had been erected. Jean-Paul explained that these were mainly occupied by holidaymakers on a seasonal basis.

'In some of them the arrangements are fairly primitive,' he said. 'But don't be nervous. Your uncle's house is not like that. In fact, according to Madame Guisard, your uncle's housekeeper, it is the last word in luxury.' He smiled at her. 'Madame Guisard is the aunt of Madame Benedict, who has the restaurant where you had lunch. That is why I am so well informed.'

Marty had to laugh. 'Thank you, Jean-Paul. I'm sure that to be forewarned is forearmed.'

'*Comment?*' He wrinkled his brow, and she realised that she had not made her meaning clear. She was casting around for another way of expressing herself, when he began to slow down. They had passed a number of tracks leading into the forest—some leading to houses, others to nature trails and picnic areas, but the track Jean-Paul was turning into was guarded by a high white gate. Marty's eyes ran over the notice on a stark white board standing beside it. '*Défense d'entrer, sous peine d'amende. Chien méchant.*' She swallowed. So trespassers on the Villa Solitaire land would be prosecuted and also had to beware of the dog. It wasn't the most welcoming of prospects. But she wasn't trespassing, she protested inwardly, she had been invited there, and she only hoped that the dog would appreciate the subtle difference. She wished very much that she had taken the precaution to telephone Uncle Jim before leaving Les Sables, but now they were here she could hardly request Jean-Paul to drive her to the nearest callbox.

Suppressing a little sigh, she prepared to climb out of the car. Jean-Paul was also out, retrieving her case which he carried over to the gate. He stood waiting for her to join him.

'You wish me to accompany you?' he asked.

Marty shook her head. In spite of her misgivings, she had a strong feeling that her reunion with Uncle Jim was likely to be an emotional one, and she did not particularly want any witnesses.

'No, thank you, Jean-Paul.' She held out her hand for him to shake. 'You've been very kind.'

He shrugged. '*Pas de quoi.*' He held on to her hand and she felt her cheeks grow warm under his intent gaze. 'You realise that I don't even know your name, although you know mine. That is hardly fair.'

'I suppose not. My name is Martina—I suppose you would say Martine.'

'Martine.' He smiled. 'It's a pretty name. And are you going to let me see you again, Martine? You cannot intend to devote the whole of your vacation to your uncle.'

Her flush deepened. 'Er—thank you, Jean-Paul. I'd like that.'

'I'll telephone you, then,' he promised. '*Au revoir*, Martine.' He walked back to the car and got in. With a hesitant hand set on the latch of the gate, Marty turned to watch him go. He swung the car round with an expert flick, and then leaned out of the window to shout back to her.

'Don't be afraid, *chérie*. The dog won't bite you—although the owner might!' And he drove off laughing.

'Thank you for nothing,' Marty muttered half under her breath. She pushed tentatively at the gate and it gave way, opening with a protesting squeal of hinges. She began to walk up the sloping sandy track, littered with pine needles and fir cones. Above her the trees seemed to close over her head, so that she appeared to be in a dim green tunnel. She stumbled slightly as her foot caught against a hidden obstacle, and paused to transfer her case to the other hand. The track had curved slightly and she could no longer see the road. A solitary house was right, she thought.

She was disturbed at the apparent change in the Uncle Jim she remembered. Yet his letter had seemed full of the old warmth and affection. Why then did he erect a high gate and warning notices at the entrance to his property? Was he afraid of thieves and vandals, or had age simply made him eccentric? The genial burly figure she remembered from childhood would have dismissed such precautions with contempt, she thought with a sigh.

She walked forward once again over the rutted path. It was very quiet in the forest. She supposed the beach must be quite close at hand, yet she could hear no sound of the sea. There was a faint whisper of a breeze in the branches above her head, and an incessant chirping of insects in the undergrowth, but as far as other human beings were concerned, she could have been alone in the world.

The track curved again, and suddenly the house was in front of her, standing in a large clearing on top of a rise, looking as inviting as it had done in the photograph. Marty paused and set the case down, wiping damp palms down the denim jeans which clung to her hips and thighs, and twitching the cheesecloth smock she wore with them into place. Her mouth felt dry and she passed her tongue nervously over her lips.

'Oh, please be glad to see me,' she whispered as she moved forward again up the rise towards the front door. 'Oh, please . . .'

She never even heard the dog come. One moment she seemed quite alone, and the next the animal was in front of her, its front legs splayed menacingly, its lip curling back in an unmistakable snarl.

Without the slightest conviction in her voice Marty said, 'Good dog. Good boy, lie down.' She wondered if she ought to extend her hand in friendship, but decided against it. The dog might misunderstand, and she might need that hand again one day.

She took another step forward and froze as the dog snarled again, then lifted its voice in a full-throated bark that held a clear warning that she was to keep her distance.

Marty glanced round nervously. Why didn't someone come? Uncle Jim, for preference, but even this Madame Guisard would do at a pinch. She tried calling out, 'Is anyone there?' first in English and then in French, but no one answered, and she felt a cold prickle of fear at the nape of her neck. Was the house deserted then except for this dog, only too aware of his role as guardian and protector? She had a feeling that any movement, even one of retreat, would be fatal. All she could do was stand there, and hope that the big animal would restrict himself to this threatening surveillance. At the same time, she was not sure how long she could go on standing there. Her legs were shaking under her suddenly, and she could feel the sun blazing down on her unprotected head, and the case weighing down almost unbearably on her arm.

She called out again, uncaring that there was now a note of panic in her voice—'Please—someone . . .'—and heard almost unbelievingly the sound of an approach, an unmistakably masculine stride, and closed her eyes with a little sob of relief. Uncle Jim—it had to be.

When she opened them again, trees, sky and house swam a little under her gaze and a droplet of sweat ran down her face. She put up her free hand and wiped her eyes because she seeemd to be suffering from the strangest illusion. The image on the snapshot in her handbag had suddenly been reproduced all over again.

She looked at the newcomer, her lips slightly parted. Tall, and very dark, and even more deeply tanned than Jean-Paul, and making no secret of it either, for all he appeared to be wearing was a pair of closely fitting white denim jeans slung low on his lean hips. A thin face with high cheekbones, and an uncompromising beak of a nose. A harsh face, belied only slightly by the sensual curve of his lower lip.

Marty took a step forward encouraged by the fact that the dog was quiet now, crouched at his feet, with one restraining hand on his collar.

She said uncertainly, 'Bernard?'

She could hardly believe it. This man was in his thirties. Had Uncle Jim been married all that time and never disclosed the fact? It seemed incredible.

She heard him give a slight intake of breath, so it seemed she had guessed right.

He said in English with only a trace of an accent, 'Who are you, and what do you want here? Didn't you read the notice?'

Dark eyes under heavy lids went over her in a kind of contemptuous dismissal that flicked Marty on the raw.

She said hotly, 'I don't call that much of a welcome.'

'I don't feel particularly welcoming. Be good enough to state your business and leave.'

Marty flung her head back and stared him straight in the eye. She said silkily, 'You may not be expecting me, Bernard, but your father is. So please take me to him.' She waited, but there was no response except a slight narrowing of the dark eyes, and a faint unpleasant smile curling his lips. 'Did you hear me, Bernard?' she asked eventually.

'Oh, I heard you, *mademoiselle*. I am just asking myself what little game you're playing. However, it seems you wanted to see me, so here I am.'

'I want to see your father ...' she began, but he interrupted, his voice cold with suppressed anger.

'*Au contraire, mademoiselle*, you said you wanted to see *Bernard*'s father. Well, I am Bernard's father.'

She stared at him. 'But you can't be! I mean ...' She put her case down and took another step forward. 'I think it's you that are playing games, *monsieur*. What are you—some sort of bodyguard? It all fits in with the gate, and the notice and the dog. Has Uncle Jim suddenly become a millionaire?'

He stood very still, and she saw his brows draw together in a swift frown. 'Whom did you say?' he asked. 'You spoke of an uncle?'

'Yes,' she said wearily, wishing that he would at least permit her to enter the house, and continue this futile conversation in the shade. She only wished that Uncle Jim would suddenly appear and put him in his place. 'My uncle —James Langton. He owns this villa.'

The tension in the air between them was suddenly almost tangible.

'You are mistaken, *mademoiselle*,' he said bleakly. 'I own this villa. Your—uncle, Monsieur Langton, sold it to me just over a year ago.'

CHAPTER TWO

MARTY stared at him, her heart beating so wildly that she had the oddest sensation that it might leap into her throat and choke her.

'But that's impossible!' she managed at last.

'*Au contraire, mademoiselle*, it is not merely a possibility, but reality.' He spoke almost wearily. 'As I suspect you knew before you ever set out on your travels. Accept my felicitations on the depth of your research and commiserations that it has not had the desired effect.'

'I don't know what you're talking about,' she said helplessly. 'But if Uncle Jim really isn't here, perhaps you can tell me where he has gone.'

The firm mouth curled slightly as if in distaste. 'You should have continued your research, *ma petite*, then you would have discovered the answer to that for yourself.'

'Please stop talking in riddles,' she begged wearily. 'I don't understand what's going on. You say Uncle Jim sold you this villa a year ago, Did he go away, then?'

The stranger paused, his dark eyes raking over her. 'Not immediately, no. Is it important?'

'Yes.' Marty fumbled at the catch of her shoulder bag. 'You see, I had a letter from him only three weeks ago asking me to come and live with him and ...'

He interrupted sharply, his frown deepening. 'Three weeks? To turn your own words against you, *mademoiselle*, that is impossible.'

'But I can show you the letter,' she began.

'I am sure you can.' His look of contemptuous derision scourged her. 'But I think it's time I called a halt to this little game you're playing. Your pretence is in the worst of bad taste under the circumstances. I suppose I can admire your determination to carry it through, but that is all I admire.'

'I don't want your admiration.' In spite of her bewilderment, Marty felt her own temper begin to rise under the lash of the man's words. How dared he treat her like this! she stormed inwardly. If she had trespassed on his property and his time then it was quite inadvertent. 'In fact, I don't want any part of you,' she went on stonily, ignoring the look of frank scepticism he sent her. 'If you'll be good enough'—she stressed the words sarcastically—'to tell me where Mr Langton has gone, then I'll be on my way.'

'Perhaps the truth will shame you into abandoning this ridiculous charade,' he said harshly. 'Jacques Langton is dead, *mademoiselle*, and has been so for the past four months. That is why I know you are a fraud, and that is why I am ordering you to leave—now.'

'Dead!' Marty repeated the word mechanically, her mind oblivious to everything else he had said. Then, as the full realisation finally dawned on her, she gave a little anguished cry. 'Dead? Oh, Uncle Jim, no!'

She gave a desperate look around her at the house, and the brooding pines and the tall inimical figure of the man confronting her, then the great golden disc of the sun came swooping down at her, and she gave a little moan and collapsed to the ground.

The sun seemed to be all about her. She felt as if she was bathed in fire. There were even slow flames forcing themselves between her lips and trickling down her throat, and she began to struggle against them, pushing them away, and pressing her hands to her mouth.

'Don't be a little fool.' She recognised the voice at once, and sat up with a gasp. 'It's only cognac. You fainted—remember?'

She was lying on a sofa inside the villa, in a long room full of light. The walls and carpeting were some pale subtle shade between cream and mushroom, and one wall was glass from floor to ceiling giving access to a paved patio. The only real colour in the room came from the abstract paintings hanging on the wall above the empty fireplace, and above the sofa where she was lying, which appeared to be the work of the same artist.

One half of her brain seemed to register these details quite coldly while the other cried out in protest as she did indeed remember only too well what had passed between them. She felt nauseated, and she knew too that she was going to cry, feeling her face begin to crumple like a child's.

But I can't, she thought agonisedly, I can't cry in front of him, even as the first sobs tore harshly at her chest. The tears were slow and scalding at first, grief and shock mingling with loneliness and disappointment as the full extent of her loss came home to her. It was something she was unable to control even though it was a degradation to expose her emotions in front of this man.

At last she sat motionless, her face buried on her arm against the cool leather of the sofa, then with a long quivering sigh she dragged herself upright on to her feet.

'I'm sorry,' she said remotely. 'I—I'll go now.'

He had been standing with his back to her, staring out of the window and she supposed she should be grateful to him for that.

'Wait.' He swung round at the sound of her voice. 'Either you're a better actress than I gave you credit for, or I have done you an injustice. Which is it? Tell me the truth.'

'I don't have to tell you anything.' She bent and picked up her bag which was lying on the floor at her feet. 'What have you done with my case?'

He walked over to her and took her chin in his hand. She wanted to snatch herself away from him, but made herself stand very still and endure his touch.

'The tears were real,' he said half to himself. 'And an actress surely would have learned to cry prettily and not allow her eyes to become swollen and her nose red.'

'Thank you,' she said ironically. 'Now may I go, please?'

'In a moment. You came here in your own good time. You will depart in mine.' He released her and walked over to the door. 'Albertine!'

A thin woman appeared so promptly that she might have been hovering on the threshold waiting for the summons.

He said in French, 'Take Mademoiselle to the bathroom, and see that she has all that she needs. She has had a great shock.'

The woman nodded, her dark eyes avid with curiosity as they rested on Marty. She tutted briskly and placed a hand on her arm, urging her towards the door.

'I don't want to use your bathroom,' Marty said tightly. 'I don't want any help from you. I just want to get away from here.'

He gave her a cool look. 'You need to wash your face before you do anything, *mademoiselle*.'

Rebellion welled up in her, but she caught sight of the housekeeper obviously relishing every minute of this passage at arms between her employer and his unexpected guest, and bit back the angry words trembling on her lips.

She accompanied the woman out of the room and into a large hall, its floor coolly tiled. A shallow flight of stairs led up to the first floor, and the woman guided Marty up these and along the gallery above to the bathroom.

Left alone in the bathroom once she had been supplied with a fresh bar of exquisitely scented soap and a small rather harsh-feeling linen towel, Marty stared around at her surroundings. At any other time, she would have been bound to appreciate the exquisite tiling of the walls and floor in shades of beige and rust and amber, as well as the magnificent appointments, including a luxurious shower cubicle, but now it was as much as she could do to run some water in the marble basin and splash it over her face and wrists. Although she hated to admit it, the touch of the water was refreshing, and by the time the woman who she realised must be the Madame Guisard that Jean-Paul had mentioned had returned, the more obvious marks of grief had vanished, although she still looked pale and red-eyed.

As they returned downstairs, Marty saw her case standing in the hall below. It looked forlorn and out of place, stationed next to a large wooden chest that was clearly an antique. As out of place as she was herself, she thought. And what had Uncle Jim had to do with all this restrained elegance?

Madame led her across the hall and tapped almost deferentially on the partially opened door to the *salon*.

'Mademoiselle is here, *monsieur*,' she annnounced, accompanying the words with a little push as if she sensed Marty's reluctance to face the new master of the house once again.

'So I see.' He was seated, his muscular limbs relaxed in one of the massive hide chairs that flanked the fireplace. 'You had better bring some tea, Albertine. That is the English stimulant, is it not, and Mademoiselle did not care for the cognac.'

'I don't want anything,' Marty protested.

'Some tea, Albertine.' He repeated without haste. He waved a hand at the chair opposite. 'Be seated, *mademoiselle*, and let us see if we can get to the bottom of this affair.'

She hesitated for a long moment, then sat down tensely on the very edge of the seat.

He waited until the door had closed behind Madame Guisard, then said in a slightly gentler tone than he had used so far, 'Is it true that you are the niece of Jacques Langton?'

'Not exactly.' Marty moistened her lips. 'He was my father's cousin,' she went on hurriedly, seeing the now familiar look of scepticism on his face. 'I—I always called him my uncle.'

'I understand. Under the circumstances I regret that I broke the news of his death to you quite so bluntly.'

'It doesn't matter,' she said quietly. 'After all, it doesn't alter anything, and I had to find out some time. There's no easy way to break that sort of news.' She took a deep breath. 'Can you tell me a little more about it?'

He gave a slight shrug. 'There is little to tell. Jacques had suffered from a weak heart for some time. He had three attacks and the last one killed him. It was very sudden and very quick. Is that what you wanted to know?'

'I suppose so,' she said after a pause. 'I'm glad he wasn't an invalid for any length of time. He would have hated it so.'

'That is true.' He leaned back in his chair, his eyes going over her from head to foot, frankly and deliberately assessing her, so that in spite of herself she felt herself flushing under his all-compassing gaze. 'What I cannot understand,' he went on after a moment, 'is why when I asked Jacques after the first attack if there was anyone in England whom I should contact, he told me there was no one. How do you explain that?'

'I wouldn't even begin to try,' she said rather hopelessly. 'Any more than I can explain why he should write to me offering me a home that was no longer his.'

'Are you sure the letter came from him?'

'Absolutely certain.'

'May I see it?'

Her handbag was no longer on the floor, but lying on the sofa. She found the letter and passed it to him. As their fingers brushed fleetingly, she was conscious of a curious tingling sensation, and her flush deepened. She tried to tell herself that it was because of her overcharged emotional state that she felt this strange new heightened awareness, but the explanation was not wholly convincing. She found herself glancing at him from beneath her lashes as he sat reading the letter and frowning a little. He seemed completely at ease, but then why shouldn't he be, in his own home? She was being idiotic. He was quite entitled to behave as he liked, but this did not stop her wishing that he would go and put a shirt on. She had never realised before what an exclusively feminine environment she seemed to have inhabited all her life. Even Mr Leslie whose secretary she had been had been a prissy, old-maidish kind of man, always rather fretfully searching for his pen and his spectacle case.

She had thought Jean-Paul was attractive, but this was before she set eyes upon this man whom even her lack of sophistication could recognise had come to terms with his own virility a long time ago, and no longer needed to prove anything about himself to anyone.

As she watched he reached for a pack of cigarettes on the table beside his chair, and selected one with a practised flick of his wrist. Even that most conventional of movements was enough to set the muscles rippling across his shoulders and chest where the dark mat of hair grew so thickly, tapering down his flat stomach to disappear inside the waistband of his pants.

'My apologies, *mademoiselle*. Do you use these things?'

With a start Marty pulled herself out of her disturbing reverie to the realisation that he was holding the pack of cigarettes out to her.

A faint smile was curving his mouth as if he was letting her know that he had been quite well aware of her scrutiny, and that her face had been an open book for the conflicting thoughts and emotions stirring within her.

A wave of colour rose to complete her betrayal as she swiftly shook her head. 'Thank you, but I don't smoke.'

'But how wise,' he said, still with that faint amusement underlying his words, and making her feel gauche and defenceless. He lit his own cigarette and blew out a cloud of pungent blue smoke before resuming his perusal of her letter. Marty bent her head and stared down at the scuff marks on her dusty sandals. She was beginning to wish that she had made no protest, no attempt to justify her presence here. At least by this time she would have been away from this place, and why the prospect of being alone and almost penniless in a strange country should seem safer than the comparative luxury of her present surroundings was far too complex a question for her to answer to her entire satisfaction in her present confused and emotional state.

She started as the door opened and Madame Guisard came back into the room carrying a tray. In spite of the strange inner conviction that the housekeeper did not approve of her for some reason, Marty could not deny that her preparations for this unwanted tea-party were well-nigh perfect. As well as the hot and fragrant tea with its attendant dish of sliced lemon, there was also a plate of enticing pastries—horns filled with cream and smooth chocolate and pastry shells filled with peaches and cherries and glazed in rich syrup. The housekeeper arranged the tray to her satisfaction on a small table and busied herself with the pouring out of the tea. Marty supposed that she considered the delicate porcelain cups and teapot too fragile to be entrusted to her own tender mercies, nor did she miss the narrow-eyed glance Madame favoured her with as she handed her the cup. And apparently the master of the house did not miss it either, in spite of his preoccupation with the letter. His voice was pitched too low for Marty to catch the words, but the tone was quite plainly dismissive and Madame Guisard left the *salon* with something of a flounce.

Now that they were alone again the silence between them seemed almost tangible, and Marty felt the tension building up inside her as she waited for him to make some comment. The initiation of any discussion was beyond her, and the fingers that held the delicate handle of her cup shook slightly as she raised her tea to her lips.

'It's incredible,' he said at last. 'I would swear that this was Jacques' handwriting, yet it must be a forgery.'

Marty's heart missed a beat and she set down her cup, staring at him wide-eyed.

'A forgery—but who on earth would do such a thing?' She caught the faint derision in the glance he bent upon her and exploded, 'You think I did it, don't you?'

'It seems the most reasonable explanation.'

'But why?' She almost wrung her hands in fury. 'What possible motive could I have for doing such a thing?'

He shrugged. 'Perhaps because you wanted to attract my attention. If so, your ploy has succeeded admirably, *mademoiselle*. I congratulate you.'

She loked at him fiercely, her small breasts rising and falling in time with her erratic breathing. 'You really must be the most abominably arrogant and conceited man it has ever been my misfortune to meet,' she said, her voice shaking. 'Do you honestly think that you're so irresistible that a woman would travel half across Europe simply to be noticed by you, because if so . . .'

'A number of women have travelled twice that distance— and shown even more determination on their arrival than you have,' he said dispassionately. 'Where you differ from them is in your unwillingness to admit that your motives for coming here are not of the purest. I can only guess that Jacques must have written to you before his death telling you to whom he had sold the villa, and your ambition led you to make the best possible use of your information.'

Ambition—motives—information? Marty's head reeled. Nothing he was saying made the slightest sense, and to her horror she felt the weakness of tears threatening to overcome her again. She couldn't break down a second time under his ironic gaze. She sprang to her feet.

'You accused me of playing games, *monsieur*, but it's you that seems to enjoy talking in riddles. But I'm afraid your snide insinuations are wasted on me. I came here hoping to find a home and someone to love me, that's all. Laughable, isn't it, and I apologise for being so naïve. But if that letter was a fraud and a hoax, then I was the victim, not the perpetrator. And I can assure you I have no desire to pander to your overwhelming ego by adding another name to your list of conquests. I'll go now. Please don't bother to show me to the door.'

She took two steps across the salon before his hand descended on her shoulder, turning her forcibly to face him.

She gasped in mingled pain and fury as his fingers bruised her flesh.

'Take your hands off me!' she raged, her balled fists lifting instinctively to strike at his bare chest.

'*Tais-toi*,' he ordered, his voice as harsh and abrupt as a blow in the face. 'Calm down for a moment, you little firebrand, and tell me something. What's my name?'

His hand snaked down and closed around both her slender wrists, holding them in a paralysing grip as he stared down into her face. He was holding her so close to him that she could feel the warmth from his half-bared body on her own skin. This new proximity was too sudden, too intimate, she found herself thinking wildly.

'I said what's my name?' The dark face came threateningly near her, his piercing eyes seeming to mesmerise her.

'How should I know?' she flung back at him. 'Don Juan, I suppose, or Casanova. They both seem eminently suitable.'

'Try Luc Dumarais.' His eyes continued to bore relentlessly into hers while the grip on her wrists increased in pressure until she thought she would be forced to cry out if he did not let her go. He seemed to be awaiting a particular response from her, but for the life of her she could not guess what it was.

'Is that supposed to mean something to me?' she asked at last.

'Perhaps. Perhaps not.' The black brows were drawn together frowningly, but to her relief that crushing grasp of her wrists had slackened. 'You don't go to the cinema?'

She shook her head, her startled eyes searching his face. 'Is that ... I mean, are you a film star?'

He gestured impatiently. 'God spare me that! I'm a director. And you? If you're another would-be actress looking for a part in my next film, you'd better confess now.'

'An actress?' She closed her eyes for a moment. 'You must be mad! I've never been on a stage in my life.' Not since, she thought achingly, that abortive chance she'd been offered as a child at school. She managed an unsteady laugh. 'I could hardly look less like an embryo film star.'

'It is no longer necessary to look like a carbon copy of Bardot,' he said drily. 'Your clothes are poor and your hair is badly cut, but with a little attention you would not be unattractive.'

She flushed angrily, pulling herself free from his slackened grasp. She was quite well aware of her own shortcomings, she thought furiously. She didn't need to have them pointed out by this arrogant Frenchman, even if he was a film director as he claimed. And she had to admit that for all she knew he could be all he said and more. Aunt Mary had considered the price of cinema seats a sinful waste of money and had reacted in horror against the permissive trend in what was being shown at a great many film centres. Within this context, all foreign films had been a particular anathema to her, and Marty had never even been allowed to watch any of the great classics of the genre shown on television.

'Well, I'm sorry to disappoint you, but I've never heard of you,' she said with childish ungraciousness, and saw his firm lips twist in wry acknowledgment.

'I believe you,' he said. 'I don't think even an experienced actress could have managed that look of total blankness when you heard my name. So I acquit you of coming here with an ulterior motive.'

'Thank you!' She concentrated as much acid as she was capable of in her tone.

'But that still does not explain the letter.' He walked back to his chair and picked it up, studying it yet again, then turning his attention to the envelope.

'The letter is undated, but there is a postmark,' he remarked at last. 'Curious. It was posted in Les Sables just over a month ago.'

Marty moved her shoulders wearily. 'Someone's idea of a cruel joke, I suppose,' she said. 'I hope whoever it is will be delighted with their success.'

'I think not,' he said abruptly. 'As I said before, no one here knew of your existence. Jacques never mentioned you, and as far as we all knew he died without kin.'

'He was always a loner,' Marty said tiredly. 'He—he travelled a great deal all his life and seemed to find it difficult to put down roots. But he always promised that when he finally made a settled home for himself, he would send for me.'

'And you believed him?'

She looked at him in bewilderment. 'Of course. Uncle Jim wouldn't lie to me.'

'I didn't mean that. I meant that you believed he would be capable of creating this stable environment that you desired so greatly. You never paused to ask yourself whether this was the right thing to ask of such a man—a loner, as you yourself have said—a nomad even. You never asked yourself whether such a leopard would be able to change his spots?'

'No, I never did.' It was shaming to have to confess her lack of perception, her stubborn refusal to accept that the doubts Aunt Mary had raised had been valid ones. She had been too ready to blame them on prejudice, and had failed to see that they were not without foundation. She cleared her throat. 'Why did Uncle Jim sell the villa to you?'

'He needed the money,' he returned with brutal frankness. 'The flower farm had been a failure, although he tried hard enough to make a success of it, and he was deeply in debt. We had met some months before when I was staying in the locality and he knew I was looking for a house, so we came to an arrangement.' His hand came out and lifted her chin gently. 'If it is any consolation to you,' he said quietly, 'he clearly intended that you should have the best. I have not altered the house at all since I moved in except to install my own furniture. It took all the money he had been able to save in a lifetime and all he could borrow as well to buy this villa.'

'But why?' Marty fought her tears. 'I didn't want—all

this. I would have been content with something far smaller
—humbler.'

'But maybe he could not,' he said. 'Perhaps a promise
made to a child assumed paramount importance in his life,
in his thinking. Perhaps when you make a dream come true
for someone, there should be no half measures. And perhaps too he knew he did not have a great deal of time left.
According to the letter, this was meant to be your in-
heritance.'

'You're talking now as if you believe Uncle Jim really did
write that letter!'

He shrugged. 'What other rational conclusion is there?
All that remains to be explained is the lapse of time between the writing, and its posting.' He paused and she saw
an intentness in his expression as if he was listening to
something. He released her and with a fierce gesture to her
to keep silence, he strode swiftly and quietly towards the
door of the *salon*, jerking it open.

Marty heard him speaking to someone in French, his
voice like a whiplash, and she quailed. Surely the austere
Madame Guisard didn't descend to listening at keyholes,
she thought, a hysterical desire to laugh welling up inside
her.

But when Luc Dumarais reappeared he was holding the
arm of a young boy, thin and dark-haired, the slenderness
of his wrists and ankles betraying how brief the journey he
had taken so far towards adolescence. His mouth set and
mutinous, he glared up at the man who was thrusting him
mercilessly towards where Marty was standing, open
mouthed.

'I have the honour to present my son Bernard, *mademoiselle*,' Luc Dumarais said tightly. 'His interest in the
matter we have been discussing leads me to think he could
shed some light on the problem that has been perplexing
us.' He picked up the letter and the envelope and held them
out to the boy, who stared at them sullenly.

'*Alors*, Bernard,' his father said almost silkily. 'Did you send this letter to Mademoiselle Langton?'

There was a long silence. Bernard's slightly sallow complexion took on a deep guilty flush. His lips parted slightly, but no sound came out.

Marty felt suddenly sorry for him. 'It's all right, Bernard,' she said, trying to sound encouraging. 'I'm sure you meant well and ...'

'I did not mean anything,' he interrupted flatly in heavily accented English. 'I found the letter in a book that Jacques gave me. I thought that I would send it, that was all.'

'How long ago did you find it?' Luc Dumarais demanded.

Bernard shrugged, his face peevish. 'I don't remember. A long time ago—just after he died.'

'And it did not occur to you that a more proper course of action would have been to give me the letter, so that I could pass it on to the lawyer who was dealing with Jacques' affairs?' Luc said coldly.

'Why should I?' Bernard flung his head back defiantly and faced his father. 'The letter was not written to you. It was not your business.'

'Or yours,' Luc Dumarais returned harshly. 'Yet you chose to make it so.'

Bernard shrugged again. 'I did not know what was in it,' he muttered defensively. 'I did not know that Mademoiselle would be fool enough to come here. Who is she?' he added. 'Jacques' mistress?'

Almost before he had finished speaking, Luc's hand shot out and slapped him across the face. The boy staggered back wincing with a gasp that was echoed by Marty's.

She whirled on Luc. 'There was no need for that, surely!'

'There was every need.' His voice sounded weary. 'Or are you accustomed to be insulted in such a manner?'

'No, of course not.' Marty was taken aback. 'But he didn't mean it.'

Luc's smile held no amusement whatsoever. 'He meant

it.' He turned and gave his son who was standing, his fingers pressed to his cheek, a long hard look. 'As he always means every word of the mischief he makes. *Pauvre* Bernard! Were you so lost for ways to anger me that you had to send all the way to England? Involve a complete stranger?'

'Well, it has been a success, *tout de même*,' the boy burst out suddenly, and Marty was horrified at the malice in his voice. 'For now this girl has come, and you will have to deal with her, *mon père*.' He turned and ran out of the room, banging the *salon* door behind him.

Marty heard Luc Dumarais swear softly under his breath before he swung back to face her.

'As you see, *mademoiselle*,' he said coldly, 'your intervention on my son's behalf was quite unnecessary. He has his own weapons.'

Marty spread her hands out helplessly in front of her. 'I'm sorry,' she said inadequately.

'There is no need,' he said impatiently. 'It is I who must apologise to you as it was my son who has brought you on this wild goose chase.'

'But why should he do such a thing?'

'You heard,' he said. 'To annoy me. To disrupt the peace I have tried to establish here. To cause me yet more problems, and eventually to prove such a thorn in my flesh that I will willingly send him back to Paris to his mother's family.'

'And you aren't prepared to do that?' Marty ventured.

'No, I am not.' Luc Dumarais stretched tiredly. He did not volunteer any further explanation and his dark face was so harsh and strained suddenly that Marty did not dare probe further.

There was a long silence. It was eventually broken by Luc, and Marty had the impression that he was forcing himself back from some bitter journey into the past. She tried to remember what Jean-Paul had said about the household while she was still under the mistaken impression that his remarks referred to Uncle Jim. He had spoken of a divorce, she thought, and also that Bernard's mother was dead. He had also given her the feeling that Bernard would not welcome her presence. But then, she thought, Bernard would not be welcoming to anyone. Brief though their meeting had been, she had sensed an air of resentment and hostility which seemed to encompass the world at large.

'Now we must decide what must be done with you.' He sounded resigned.

'That's easily settled.' Marty tried to shut out of her mind the chilling realisation of just how much she had staked on this trip and the pitiful amount of money now left to her. 'I—I shall return to England. There really isn't any need to concern yourself . . .'

'Don't be a fool.' His voice bit at her. 'My son was to blame for bringing you here. The responsibility now rests with me. Just how do you propose to return to England? Did you buy a return ticket for the ferry?'

'No,' she admitted. 'But that's no problem.' She tried to sound careless—a seasoned traveller, and saw his eyes narrow speculatively as he looked her over.

'You have travellers' cheques?' he asked pleasantly. 'Or are your resources restricted to those few francs you have in your bag?'

For a moment she was stunned, then she blazed at him. 'You dared—you actually dared to look in my bag?'

'Yes, I dared,' he said calmly. 'I wished to check your passport and make sure you had a right to the identity you were claiming. Or did you think I would trustingly let any strange waif into my house, merely because she professed kinship with a man no longer alive to support or deny her claim? It seemed to me that you had planned only on a one-way trip.'

'The more fool I,' she said tightly. 'But it really isn't any of your concern. I'm sure if I really had been an actress with an eye on a part in your latest film you would have thrown me out without a second thought. Just because

Martina Langton, starlet, doesn't exist, Martina Langton, secretary, doesn't require your charity either.'

'There are arrangements you can make? Relatives in England you can cable for money?'

Marty suppressed a wry smile as she visualised Aunt Mary's reaction to any such demand.

'No, there's no one,' she acknowledged quietly. 'But I'll manage. I'm quite capable of working, you know, and Les Sables is a seaside resort. I can get a job at one of the hotels—waiting at tables perhaps, or as a chambermaid.'

'Les Sables is a small resort. Most of the hotels are family businesses and do not make a habit of employing outsiders, especially foreigners. Any casual work available has already been snapped up by students,' he said unemotionally. 'What other ideas have you?'

'None,' she was provoked into admitting. She lifted her chin defiantly and looked at him. 'But I'll think of something.'

'I have already thought of something.' His voice was cool and almost dispassionate. 'You can remain here.'

CHAPTER THREE

'THAT,' Marty said after a heart-thumping pause, 'is the last thing I shall do.'

She spoke carefully, anxious to keep any betraying quiver out of her voice. Her pulses were behaving very oddly all of a sudden, and she wanted to wipe her damp palms on her jeans, but she restrained herself. The last thing she wanted was to let Luc Dumarais know the turmoil his suggestion had thrown her into.

Frantic thoughts began to gallop through her head. If she screamed, would Madame Guisard hear—and if she heard, would she bother to take any action? Could she manage to get past Luc Dumarais to the door? Thanks to Bernard, it was shut. Would he catch her before she could get it open and make her escape? Then there was the dog. Her mouth felt suddenly dry, and she moistened her lips with the tip of her tongue.

'*Mon dieu*,' he said very softly. 'It's really true. The prototype English virgin, spying rapists behind every bush. Calm yourself, *ma petite*,' he went on, his mouth twisting sardonically. 'I've never been forced to resort to rape yet. And if I wanted a little adventure, believe me I wouldn't choose an inexperienced child as a partner.'

Marty felt the hot blood invade her cheeks. 'You're quite wrong,' she protested without conviction. 'I wasn't thinking ...'

'Don't lie,' he said. 'Has no one told you, *mon enfant*, that your face is a mirror to your thoughts? Did you really imagine that you had inflamed my passions to such an extent that I could not bear to let you go?'

'You,' she said very distinctly, 'are quite the most loathsome man I have ever met.'

'But then I would say such encounters have been rather limited, have they not? Nor is it exactly courteous to describe a prospective employer as loathsome.'

'You're not my employer. Nothing would prevail on me to work for you,' Marty declared tremblingly.

'No? But do you imagine you have a great deal of choice?' he enquired. 'You haven't sufficient money to eat, and travel to a larger place to find work—even supposing there was anyone willing to give you a job. You have no relatives or friends to help you, on your own admission, and I should warn you that the authorities do not look kindly on indigent foreigners.'

'How dare you call me indigent! I'm a trained secretary.'

'So I read in your passport,' he said almost negligently. 'I should not otherwise be offering you work.'

Marty gave a gasp of utter frustration. No matter what she said, he seemed to have an answer.

'Oh, this is ridiculous!' she declared. 'I—I'm going.'

She tried to march past him to the door, but his hand closed on her arm detaining her. She was aware of an almost overwhelming impulse to forget her upbringing and sink her teeth into his tanned flesh.

'I advise against it,' he said infuriatingly, almost as if she had voiced the thought aloud. 'I can promise you that you would not enjoy the inevitable reprisals.'

She stood very still, her eyes downcast, conscious only of the firm pressure of his hand upon her arm.

'Will you let me go, please?' she asked politely.

'Will you stop turning my *salon* into a battleground?' he returned, but he released her arm. 'You are in no fit state to discuss anything rationally at the moment. You have had a number of shocks today, which I regret. At least let me make amends by offering you a meal and a room for the night. In the morning you may feel better disposed to listen to what I have to say to you.'

'I doubt that very much,' she muttered. 'All I really want

to do is get away from this place.'

'Then your most sensible course of action is to earn sufficient money to make this possible,' he said unemotionally. 'You would not find me ungenerous in the matter of wages. In any case, earnings in France are higher than in England.'

There was an awful kind of logic in what he said, Marty told herself despairingly. For a moment, she toyed with the idea of asking him to advance her the fare home on the understanding that she would repay him when she got back home and found another job. But she herself could see the flaws in this. For one thing, with unemployment running rife, she had no real guarantee she would find another job very easily. And when she did, she would need somewhere to live, and had little idea how much she would have to pay for rent, and heating, not to mention her food and clothes. What money would she have to repay anyone?

An involuntary sigh broke from her lips. He had not exaggerated when he had said she was in no state to consider his offer. She wasn't just physically tired from her days of travel. She felt emotionally battered as well, her grief and disappointment at what she had discovered at the Villa Solitaire now being joined by a very real fear of what the future might hold. She had destroyed what fragile security she had had to snatch at a shadow. It had been the first reckless act she had ever committed, this journey to France, and it had ended in disaster.

And as in a kind of dream she heard Luc Dumarais summon the housekeeper and order her to escort her to a guest room, it occurred to her with a little shiver of disquiet that this might only be the beginning of the disaster ...

In spite of her forebodings, Marty fell asleep on the bed Madame Guisard somewhat grudgingly made up for her. The room itself was charming, with its white-painted walls, contrasting with the smooth modern lines of the furniture, and the deep velvety green of the fitted carpet. There were no curtains at the windows, but Marty had grown accustomed to using shutters, and she was used too to managing the long rather hard bolster that fitted under the bottom sheet in place of a pillow. Sleep when it came was dreamless, and she felt oddly refreshed when she woke to find the shadows lengthening in the room, and Madame Guisard bending over to tell her stiffly that dinner was on the point of being served.

Adjoining her room was a tiny cubicle containing a shower, a handbasin and the ubiquitous bidet. As she hurriedly rinsed her face and hands in the basin, and dragged a comb through her sleep-tousled hair, Marty wondered whether she ought to have made the effort to change for dinner. But a swift mental review of the clothes she had brought with her soon convinced her it would only be foolish. She found herself wondering whether Luc Dumarais would subscribe to convention sufficiently to put on a shirt before sitting down to dinner. After a final slightly disparaging glance at herself in the mirror, she went out of her room and downstairs to the hall where she hesitated, wondering where she would find the dining room.

As she stood there, Luc Dumarais walked out of the salon and stood watching her, his dark face enigmatic. He was wearing close-fitting dark trousers, and though he was tieless, his frilled white shirt was immaculately white. A dark blue velvet jacket hung casually over his shoulders. He looked totally and arrogantly masculine, and Marty felt the force of his dark attraction reach out and take her by the throat. She swallowed, every instinct urging her to deny these new and troublous feelings which were invading her tranquillity.

She was defiantly glad she had made no effort to change. It would have been humiliating if he had interpreted such an action as an attempt by her to persuade him of her own femininity. The casualness of jeans and a top made her feel less vulnerable.

'I have decided that we will eat outside tonight. It's a perfect evening,' he said. 'Would you care for an *aperitif*?'

'No—I mean—yes, I suppose so,' she said, feeling un-utterably gauche.

'What do you drink?' he enquired.

She was tempted to reply, 'A glass of sherry—once a year for the Queen's speech,' and see what his reaction was, but she controlled herself.

'What do you recommend?' she countered brightly.

'Perhaps you should try a *pineau*,' he said. 'It's the local aperitif, and you probably won't have come across it in England.'

How very true, Marty thought, as she followed him into the *salon*. He left her there with a quick polite word of apology while he went to fetch the drinks, and she wandered over to the glass doors that led out to the patio. A table set with a white linen cloth had been placed there, and Marty noticed with a sinking heart that place settings had only been laid for two. It appeared that Bernard would not be joining them, and she was going to have to suffer a dinner *tête-à-tête* with the master of the house—the very last thing she wanted under the circumstances. She gave a little barely perceptible sigh. The setting, the warm summer night, and the man who was soon to join her were all of the stuff that dreams were made on, and the sooner she remembered that she was prosaic Marty Langton, the better it would be for her. She had listened to the other girls who worked in her office gossiping about their boy-friends, but none of them had ever warned her that you could be physically attracted to a man you did not even like. She'd imagined there would be a safe pattern to these relationships—an enjoyment of a man's company leading steadily on to warmer, more intimate feelings in the fullness of time.

But Luc Dumarais did not fit into any pattern that she had ever conceived, even in her wildest dreams. He was quite simply beyond her scope, and it worried her to realise how much of her thoughts he was beginning to monopolise.

'Martine.' She turned with a little start, to find that he had come silently back into the room and was standing close behind her holding out a glass to her.

'*A votre santé,*' he said rather mockingly, raising his own glass in salute.

She bent her head, muttering an embarrassed, 'Cheers,' and sipped at her drink which in spite of the fact that it was icy cold, spread a new and welcome warmth through her body. Its flavour was sweet and rather rich, and she smiled at him with rather shy appreciation.

'It's good.'

He inclined his head in acknowledgment. 'Shall we take our drinks outside?' he suggested.

The heat was not as intense as it had been earlier now that evening was approaching, and the merest whisper of a breeze came sighing through the clustering pines only yards from the house to disturb the stillness of the warm air.

César was lying on the patio, his head sunk on his paws. He lifted his head and barked as Marty appeared, but at a sharp word from his master he resumed his somnolent pose.

'Are you frightened of dogs?' Luc Dumarais held the chair for Marty to sit down.

'I'm not really used to them,' she answered truthfully.

He smiled slightly. 'César will soon come to accept your presence here.' He lifted a water jug from the table and added some water to the liquid in his glass, watching it appraisingly as it turned cloudy.

He spoke, Marty thought indignantly, as if it was all cut and dried that she was going to stay and work for him. She was just about to voice her thought when Madame Guisard appeared with the tureen of soup that constituted the first course, and she had perforce to save her comments for later.

'Is Bernard not joining us?' she asked tentatively as she picked up her spoon.

Luc's dark brows drew together. 'He is eating in his room,' he said briefly. His tone did not encourage any further discussion, so Marty let the matter drop. She recalled Jean-Paul telling her that afternoon that Bernard had only come to live with his father a year ago. It seemed that even in that short period the relationship between them had deteriorated drastically. And she still wasn't clear about Bernard's motives for posting Uncle Jim's letter as he had done. It seemed such a pointless thing to have done. Yet, she supposed philosophically, at least through his action she had learned that Uncle Jim had died, however painful the knowledge was. At least she now knew she had nothing to hope for, and that she had to put that childish dream of loving security which Uncle Jim had inculcated behind her for ever.

Had it really been a burden to him, she wondered, as she drank the delicately flavoured vegetable soup, that rash promise he had made to her all those years ago? The thought grieved her almost as much as the news of his death had done. She could imagine him becoming increasingly desperate as the years went by, and there seemed no way to redeem his promise, then this final reckless splurge on this villa he could not really afford. But even then he had hesitated to send for her, as if aware that it was all going to go wrong for him. Why else had he written the letter and not posted it? And his forebodings had proved only too real, it seemed, and she sighed imperceptibly as she laid down her spoon.

'You look sad again,' Luc Dumarais remarked as the fish, cooked in cream and mushrooms, was set in front of them. 'Is the food not to your liking?'

'Oh no, it's magnificent.' Marty glanced up startled. She had not realised he was observing her so closely. 'I—I was just thinking about Uncle Jim.'

He shrugged. 'That is natural. I hope these thoughts will persuade you to act sensibly.'

'What do you mean?' she asked guardedly.

'I should have thought it was obvious. Jacques must have had a deep concern for you to act as he did. Can you imagine his reactions now if he knew you were alone, without friends or money, refusing help when it was offered?'

She bent her head. 'I think, like myself, he would have wanted to know a little more about what that help entailed before committing himself,' she said in a low voice.

'You surely don't still suspect that I have designs upon your virtue?' His brows rose. 'Please believe, Martine, that I do not steal from cradles. And there are moments when you seem hardly older than Bernard.'

'No, I don't suspect—that.' She felt that betraying colour rise in her cheeks again and prayed that he would not notice. Was it any wonder, she asked herself bitterly, that he had written her off as another gauche adolescent? 'But—was it some kind of domestic work you had in mind or ...'

'*Diable!*' He was laughing openly now. 'Albertine would have my blood if I tried to interfere in her arrangements. No, I thought I had made it clear that it was your secretarial ability that interested me—or at least that was the first thing.'

Anxious grey eyes met his and his smile widened. 'What are you thinking now, I wonder? Whatever it is, *mon enfant*, you are wrong. I need a companion for Bernard. The long vacation is ahead of us, and I have to work on a new script so I shall not be able to give him the time or the attention he so badly needs. On the other hand, I do not wish him to be left to his own resources. He is unpredictable at the best of times. When bored——' He lifted a shoulder.

Marty stared at him. 'And do you really think for one moment that my presence would make the slightest difference?' She tried to smile. 'I'm a complete stranger to him. We don't even speak each other's language very fluently. Surely he must have some friends that you could invite.'

'Unfortunately, no.' A look of strain crossed the dark

face. 'While he was living in Paris, he was permitted to associate with a group much older than he was—a group which exercised much influence on Bernard, little of it good. I have forbidden any further association with these people. Since then, he has made no effort to make other friends.'

'I see,' Marty said slowly. It was not a happy picture that Luc Dumarais had painted, and she could well imagine Bernard's reaction if she was foisted on him. On the other hand, if he was cut off from all those he had thought of as his friends, he would undoubtedly be lonely, as she was herself. An antagonistic thirteen-year-old boy was not her ideal choice of a companion, but perhaps beggars in lone-liness could not be choosers.

She cleared her throat. 'You said something about secre-tarial work too.'

'Yes.' Luc Dumarais' eyes never left her face. 'As I said, I am working on a new script. We hope to go into pro-duction in the autumn, so time is of the essence to me. I need to get at least a workable treatment to my producer and other colleagues in the next week or two. I was think-ing of bringing a secretary from Paris, but if you decide to stay, there will be no need for that.'

'And how long would the job continue?'

He shrugged. 'Shall we say until the script is finished—or you have earned sufficient money to pay your fare home—whichever happens sooner.'

He could not have sounded more businesslike or dismis-sive, and this was what she wanted, so why should his tone prove so hurtful? She pushed her plate away with hands that shook a little. The gesture was not lost on him, and his voice gentled a little.

'Sleep on it, Martine,' he suggested. 'And let me have your decision in the morning.'

'Very well,' she agreed almost inaudibly, and was thank-ful when Madame Guisard reappeared with the next course—chicken, in a sauce redolent of wine and herbs.

It was delicious, but as far as Marty was concerned, she might have been eating reconstituted sawdust.

The sun was sinking behind the pines, and there was a new chill in the air, making her shiver involuntarily.

This house had well been named Solitaire, she thought. Apart from its seclusion, its former owner Uncle Jim had been a solitary man, and the present household seemed to operate in a curious isolation from each other. Her first impressions of Bernard had not been in his favour, but a sudden wave of sympathy went over her as she wondered what it must have been like for him, being torn away at a vulnerable age from the life he was used to, and brought to this remote corner with a father who clearly had little idea of his needs, and less time for them. And there was Luc Dumarais himself. A public man, because of his career, but demanding an intensely private life, judging by the seclusion he had chosen. He had one failed marriage behind him, but that surely did not mean he had forsworn the company of women for ever.

She stole a glance at him, confident that his attention was fixed on his plate. He was far from being the handsome Frenchman of convention. The planes of his face were too harshly drawn, the rugged lines of nose and chin too firmly insisted on for that. But that in no way diminished his dark attraction, and the frankly sensual curve of his mouth hardly denoted a man who lived a celibate existence.

'Do you read character from faces, Martine?'

She almost choked on the forkful of chicken she had just placed in her mouth.

'Because if you do, I hope that you won't leap to too many hasty conclusions,' he went on.

Marty felt utterly mortified to have been caught staring at him like an impressionable schoolgirl.

'I beg your pardon,' she said stiltedly.

He looked directly at her then, and there was an odd expression in his eyes that she thought might have been a sort of kind pity.

'You are very young, aren't you,' he said, and her mortification was complete. She made herself go on eating because she was hungry, and she supposed resentfully that he would see this as yet another sign of her youth. And yet she had never considered she was young for her age. The other girls who worked at the office had always treated her as if she was much older than she actually was, nor had her aunt ever made any concessions towards childhood or adolescence. And earlier there had been Jean-Paul who had made it perfectly clear that he regarded her as a woman. So why was it just this man who could make her feel so juvenile and vulnerable? she wondered almost despairingly.

And would seeing him every day—working with him, being part of his household make their relationship any easier, or would it simply complicate matters still further? she asked herself, but no satisfactory answer seemed to be forthcoming.

She stole a glance at him, and saw him take a surreptitious look at the plain platinum watch he wore on his wrist. She bit her lip, feeling in the way. Probably his plans for the evening had not included entertaining her to dinner, she thought guiltily, laying down her knife and fork.

She only picked at the crême caramel that Madame Guisard served as a dessert and declined the coffee altogether on the somewhat mendacious grounds that it might keep her awake. Whatever made her think she was going to be able to sleep anyway—no matter what she drank or refrained from drinking?

'Are you tired?' He looked at her, his eyebrows raised interrogatively.

'Yes—I think I would like to go to my room,' she said hurriedly, remembering that swift glance at his watch, and wondered if that was a look of relief in his eyes as he turned to Madame Guisard who had come to clear the table and instructed her to see that mademoiselle had everything she needed for the night.

'Certainly, *monsieur*.' Madame seemed to find the idea less than entrancing. 'I have already unpacked Mademoiselle's case,' she added, giving Marty a sidelong glance which managed to convey she had been unimpressed by her findings. And it was true that the clothes she had brought with her were very different from the couture garments that Luc Dumarais' female guests usually brought with them, Marty decided rather sadly. Madame probably considered that denim and cheesecloth was a considerable letdown after the *crêpe de chine* and cashmere she was accustomed to.

Luc Dumarais shrugged as he refilled his own coffee cup, and produced the inevitable pack of Gauloises. 'I leave such domestic details to you, Albertine,' he said in a slightly bored tone.

Marty got up from her chair, feeling awkward. She said haltingly. 'Goodnight, *monsieur*—and thank you.'

He had also risen, extending his hand to her, and after a moment's hesitation, she allowed her fingers to be encompassed by his in the normal courteous ritual of leavetaking. For that was all it was, and she was a fool to imagine anything different, or to let that shiver of awareness go through her at the pressure of his hand on hers.

'Goodnight, Martine. Sleep well.' His dark eyes went over her broodingly. 'We will talk again tomorrow, *hein*?'

'Yes,' she said, and tried to smile. 'Tomorrow.'

Which was usually an optimistic word, she thought, as she followed Madame's rigid back through the house and upstairs to her room. So why did she feel so sure that with the morning's light, all her troubles would just be beginning?

She was thankful when the door closed behind Madame Guisard whom she had quietly assured she had everything she required for the night. It occured to her while she was making this assurance that if she had lacked everything from a nightgown to a tube of toothpaste, she would have made do somehow rather than ask Madame for her assistance. She did not have to enquire, she thought rather grimly, who had laid her shabby gingham nightdress across the bed in a way that would have done justice to a Janet Reger creation, but merely drew attention to the shortcomings of a garment which had always relied more on practicality than on glamour for its appeal. And she couldn't help wishing that there had been at least one set of chiffon and lace camiknickers for Madame to place in the waiting chest of drawers instead of much laundered chain store undies.

When the woman had gone, after bidding her a stiff, 'Bonne nuit', Marty walked across and stood staring at herself disparagingly in the full length mirror on the wall. Really there was little wonder that Luc Dumarais had wanted to get their tête-à-tête dinner over and be off on his own pursuits, she thought impatiently, condemning the slight wistfulness she saw in the depths of her grey eyes. She was on the thin side of slender, and the rather boyish clothes she was wearing did nothing to promote an illusion of lush femininity. She ran her hands over her hipbones, grimacing a little at their prominence, while her breasts, she thought somewhat unjustly, were practically non-existent.

Her hair was all right—still thick and glossy with health like a new chestnut, but its styling—fringed across her forehead and curving gently round her face—had hardly changed at all since she was a child. It was by no means unbecoming, but it wouldn't send Vidal Sassoon into a swoon of admiration either, and Marty found herself wondering uneasily why this new self-consciousness was suddenly making itself felt. She had always known that she wasn't a raving beauty, but had considered that she was ordinarily attractive, and long sessions of soul and body searching in front of mirrors were not at all her scene.

She found she was pushing impatiently at her hair, lifting it back to show her ears, dragging it back from her face with both hands to see if the harder line made her look older, more sophisticated. Then as realisation dawned, she let her hands fall motionless to her sides and stood staring at herself with frank horror.

'You're going mad,' she whispered to herself. 'You're behaving like a lunatic because you've met a man who's different from anyone you've ever encountered before. You don't even know if you like him—and you certainly don't know if you can trust him, so why the sudden concern over the way you look? He's a famous man—a film director, and the queue of willing women probably forms on the right. But that does not—*not* mean that he's asking you to join it.'

With a last derisive glance at her reflection, she walked across the room and threw herself down on the bed. Common sense told her that she ought to undress and shower, or at least close her shutters against the ever-hungry mosquitoes, yet she didn't move.

She had to rationalise this thing out, she told herself. If she was going to stay here and earn the money for her journey home, and at the moment there seemed few other possibilities, then she would be laying up nothing but trouble for herself if she started viewing her employer in anything other than a purely business light. And what was the matter with her anyway? She had never fantasised about film and television personalities like so many of her contemporaries. Her room at home had never been swamped with posters depicting the latest idol—not that Aunt Mary would ever have permitted such a thing anyway, she thought wryly. Nor had she ever had the slightest patience with girls who developed embarrassing crushes on their bosses. But then in justice, what temptation had there been for her from Mr Leslie with his anxiously pedantic fussing over the only correct way to prepare abstracts from deeds?

She rolled over on to her stomach, resting her chin on her folded arms, and gazing unseeingly at the window. Her every instinct seemed to be warning her to get away while she still had the chance, but wasn't she just being overly-dramatic?

Luc Dumarais had offered her a temporary home and a job principally because he felt sorry for her, and because he felt some sense of responsibility for his son's action in bringing her there. As far as he was concerned, that was all there was to it, and he would probably be both amused and horrified if he had the least suspicion of the wild thoughts that were beginning to dominate her mind.

He had told her to her face that she was very young, Marty thought, her teeth gritted. And that was how he undoubtedly saw her—as another child like the surly Bernard to be protected, even in spite of herself. Only she didn't somehow see Luc Dumarais as the protective type. Speaking from the depths of my vast experience, she added ironically to herself.

She gave a little disgusted groan. Why couldn't she be honest and admit that a man like Luc Dumarais was an enigma, and this was probably the basis of his attraction for her—that, and his all too potent masculinity.

A fly buzzed in through the window and swooped towards her recumbent figure. With an exclamation Marty sat up, swiping it away with her hand. She had to fasten those shutters otherwise every flying insect over a ten-mile radius would be coming to join her.

She got up and went over to the window, reaching for the hook which fastened the shutters back when they were not in use, and realised for the first time that her room was at the front of the house. Moreover there was a car parked there—a small, smart Citroën. She stared down at it, her brows puckering a little. Somehow this had not been the type of car she would have visualised Luc Dumarais driving. She could see him behind the wheel of something big and sleek and powerful.

Oh, for heaven's sake, she muttered impatiently to herself as she jerked the shutter towards her. Are you even going to stand around day-dreaming about the kind of car he drives now?

She was reaching for the other shutter when she heard voices below. She peeped cautiously out and saw that Luc had come out and was standing by the car. But he was not alone. There was a woman with him—tall and slim with dark hair drawn back into a smooth chignon. She was wearing a sleeveless dress in some neutral shade—beige or coffee, it was difficult to judge in the fading light—but cut with expensive chic. She wore a number of bracelets on one arm and they jangled audibly as she smilingly tossed Luc a bunch of car keys, with an added remark uttered in too low a voice for Marty to catch.

But everything—the gesture, the smile, even the way she stood, her body almost touching his—spoke of a long established intimacy, and of a sophistication which would make Luc Dumarais' dominating virility a challenge to be enjoyed.

And as if to set the seal on the relationship, Marty saw Luc Dumarais draw her to him, one hand on her hip, before bending to brush her lips with the light kiss of deep familiarity. Then he released her to open the passenger door of the car and help her in, before walking round to the driver's side, tossing the keys lightly up and down in his hand. After unlocking the door he straightened again, to shrug his arms into the jacket which he was still wearing loosely slung round his shoulders, and as if suddenly conscious of the scrutiny from above, he looked up.

Their eyes met as Marty froze with embarrassment. To be caught apparently spying on him, especially in those particular circumstances, was the ultimate humiliation, she thought wildly, dragging at the shutter which was, of course, stuck and refused to move immediately.

She glanced downwards again and saw that he was standing, his hands resting lightly on his hips, watching her frenzied tuggings, and even at that range she could tell he was smiling.

'Do you need any help?' he called, making no effort to disguise the mockery in his voice, and Marty saw his companion's face appear at the passenger window, also staring up, faint bewilderment being replaced by a surprised frown as she registered Marty's presence.

'No.' Marty gave a despairing heave at the shutter, and sighed with relief as it moved at last. 'Thank you,' she added belatedly, and saw him give a casual, almost derisive wave as he got into the car and started the engine.

Marty stood in the darkened room, trying to control her hurried breathing. Yes, of course, she was panting because of the effort she had been forced to make with the shutter, but that was far from being all of it.

Idiot! she lashed herself silently. You've known all along that there must be a woman. With a man like that there would have to be—and probably not just one either.

All the same, being aware of something and having it publicly demonstrated were very different things, she thought as she collected her toilet things and started for her little bathroom.

Luc Dumarais' concern about the time during dinner was explained now, and perfectly understandable, Marty thought, recalling wryly his companion's smooth, confident but understated beauty. It was not to be expected that her company would be preferred, even as a novelty, to that of such a glamorous example of a woman of the world. Perhaps he had also been relieved when Marty had taken herself off to her room, because that meant he would not be pressganged into any premature explanations of her presence in his house. Although she had ruined all that with her performance with the shutter.

She gave a little groan, as she shed the last of her clothes and stepped under the shower. She hoped that Monsieur Dumarais—it was safer to think of him that way than Luc, she decided—would not imagine she had done it on purpose, or that she had been deliberately prying into his private affairs, a turn of phrase which made her wince inwardly as she turned her body under the warm water, enjoying the refreshment of it on her skin.

And she hoped too that his—she hesitated—friend's discovery that he had a strange girl staying in his house would not have done anything to spoil their evening.

Yes, she reiterated to herself as she wrapped the towel round her wet body, she did hope that. She hoped that Luc Dumarais and his—girl-friend—mistress—fiancée? would have a wonderful evening together, and a wonderful night as well if that was what they wanted, and this sudden strange pain that seemed to be tearing her apart was loneliness and fear and grief for Uncle Jim in whom she had invested so much hope and faith.

It was not—and she pressed her hands almost convulsively against her small breasts—it could not—it must not be jealousy.

CHAPTER FOUR

HER sleep that night was restless and troubled, disturbed
by strange unhappy dreams. She awoke several times, aware
that her eyes were stinging and that there was a harsh pain
in her throat, and that the bolster beneath her cheek was
damp. For a while she tossed and turned, toying with the
idea of making her way to the kitchen and preparing some
kind of hot drink, but in the end she rejected the notion. For
one thing, she had no idea where the kitchen was, and the
thought of blundering round a strange house in the dark
held no appeal whatsoever. Someone would be bound to
hear her—in all probability Madame Guisard, who certainly wouldn't welcome any kind of intrusion in her
domain, according to what Luc Dumarais had said, and
particularly not a midnight one. And thirdly there was the
dog César to whom she was also clearly an intruder, and
who might be let free to roam the house at night for all she
knew. Three very good reasons for remaining where she
was, and hoping that deeper sleep and more placid dreams
would still the ache in her heart.

It was the feeling of utter rejection which was so hard
to bear, she thought, turning on to her side and pummelling
the bolster into a more amenable shape for her flushed
cheek to rest against. She couldn't remember the dreams in
any detail, but she knew they were all connected with this
—with doors closing, and people turning away and a soul-
wrenching sense of loss and deprivation. Just before she
had woken up in tears, she had dreamed about Uncle Jim
and that she was a child again, sitting on his knee while his
hand stroked her hair and his voice gently promised that—
one day—there would be a very different future for them
both.

And it was no comfort, no comfort at all to know that she was here in the house where that future had been meant to happen. It had all gone terribly wrong—so wrong that Uncle Jim had even denied her existence. Perhaps he had done so deliberately, wanting to save her the grief that the knowledge of his death would bring, she thought, or maybe he had been afraid that she would use her precious savings for a futile journey to attend his funeral. From what she could remember of him, he had never approved of funerals, and a smothered sob rose in her throat at the recollection.

She fell asleep again at last, as sheer misery threatened to engulf her once more. She had always believed that her life with Aunt Mary had taught her a certain philosophy, but she knew very differently now. Nothing she had ever experienced—not even her mother's death all those years ago—had prepared her for this current trough of insecurity and isolation.

When she opened her eyes again, sunlight was forcing its way into the room through the shutters, and she lay quite still for a moment, assimilating her surroundings and wondering what had woken her.

Then she heard a movement in the room, quite close at hand, and sat up, her heart thumping, clutching the covers against her chest. She certainly wasn't prepared for the sight of Bernard's hunched figure occupying the high-backed white painted chair by the window.

'What are you doing here?' she asked incredulously.

'I am here to tell you that I am sorry,' he said slowly and carefully, avoiding her bewildered gaze.

'Sorry?' she echoed, pushing the hair out of her eyes.

'*Mais oui*,' he nodded. 'I am sorry that I made you come here. I did not intend that.'

'No,' Marty said roundly. 'You really meant to make your father angry. Well, if it's any consolation to you—he is.'

Bernard shrugged indifferently. 'That I know. But you I have made unhappy, and that I did not intend.' He flushed. 'I did not sleep so good last night, and I heard you crying,' he explained in a low voice.

'I see.' Marty felt her cheeks burning. As if things weren't bad enough, it now seemed that she was to have Bernard feeling sorry for her.

He gave her a speculative look. 'You are angry that I heard you? It was not my fault. I occupy the next room, and I did not sleep.'

'Your conscience was troubling you, presumably,' Marty suggested acidly.

'*Comment?*'

'It doesn't matter.' She sighed. 'I accept your apology, Bernard.'

'I am pleased,' he said without the slightest evidence of pleasure. 'So now you will go, *n'est-ce pas?*'

'Go?' Marty stared at him. 'Go where?'

He gestured. 'To your residence. To Angleterre—wherever you wish. Is not so?' When she did not reply immediately, he continued, 'Jacques said you would live here with him, but that is no longer possible, so you must go.'

'Have you spoken to your father this morning?' Marty asked.

A sullen expression came into Bernard's eyes. '*Pourquoi?*'

'Because if you have, he must surely have told you of his plans.'

'Plans?' said Bernard. 'What is this of plans?'

The glimmer of suspicion within Marty grew to a flame. His refusal to meet her eye, the way he answered her questions with other questions all indicated that Bernard knew far more of what had passed between herself and Luc Damarais than he was prepared to admit, for some reason.

She shrugged. 'Oh, nothing important,' she said vaguely. 'You'd better go back to your own room now. I'm going to get up.'

Bernard rose to his feet slowly and reluctantly, digging his hands into the pockets of his dressing gown. It was maroon in colour and clearly an expensive garment, but it was too large for him, emphasising the slenderness of his wrists and the boyish fragility of his shoulders. It made him look oddly vulnerable in spite of the sulky set to his mouth, and the unchildishly veiled eyes.

'After *le petit déjeuner*—you will be leaving then?' he asked, staring down at the carpet.

Marty shrugged again. 'Perhaps,' she replied. 'Perhaps not.' She tried a tentative smile. 'Would—would you like me to stay, Bernard?'

She expected a flat denial and had already braced herself to receive it, so his hesitation was a surprise, as if her question had caught him unprepared. He walked across the room to the door. As he reached for the handle, she prompted him again. 'Or do you want me to go?'

It was his turn to shrug, his small face suddenly hard and hostile under the tangle of black hair.

'I think if you stay, you will be sorry,' he said, and went out of the room.

Marty leaned back against the bolster with a little sigh. One of her last coherent thoughts the previous night had been that Bernard's attitude would have a major influence on her decision whether to remain at Solitaire or take a chance on working and hitch-hiking her way back to Britain. True, she had not expected him to accept her presence with open arms, but she had not anticipated the warning that had been implicit in his parting words. Nor had he answered her question, she thought soberly. He had merely said she would be sorry if she stayed, but not that *he* would make her sorry. So what could he have meant?

She scrambled out of bed, and found fresh underwear and a white sleeveless top with a deep square neck. Looking up at the cloudless sky as she opened the shutters, she knew that it was going to be another scorching day, and she gave a little sigh. How different everything might have been. Working each day in her drab office, going back each night to her aunt's coldness, she had dreamed of a house like this, bathed in sunshine, only a stone's throw from the sea.

She showered hurriedly and dressed, dragging a comb through her hair, and thanking heaven for its normal healthy sheen. Then she thrust her feet into heelless sandals and went downstairs.

She could hear the sound of a vacuum cleaner being vigorously wielded in the *salon*, and peeping round the door, saw Madame Guisard, a voluminous flowered overall covering her neat dark dress.

The housekeeper saw her almost at once, and switched of the cleaner.

'Puis-je vous aider, mademoiselle?' The words were civil enough, but the tone of voice conveyed total indifference to all or any of Marty's wants.

Madame Guisard, Marty decided, was yet another person keenly anticipating her departure for some reason. But that could merely be because another presence in the house meant extra work for her. Perhaps she treated all Luc Dumarais' guests in this offhand manner, and he overlooked the eccentricity because of her undoubted skill as a cook.

She made herself smile. 'I was wondering about breakfast,' she began, and was brusquely interrupted.

'Un instant, s'il vous plaît.' Madame unplugged the cleaner and began to wind the flex, clearly displeased at the interruption.

'Oh, please,' Marty said. 'I didn't mean to get in the way of the housework. Please finish what you were doing,' she added rather desperately in French as the housekeeper continued implacably to collect up her cloths and tin of polish. 'If you'll show me where the things are, I could make my own breakfast perhaps.'

'Ce n'est pas votre affaire, mademoiselle.'

Marty remembered too late what Luc Dumarais had said about Madame brooking no interference in her domestic concerns. It seemed that even such a basic process as uniting a few slices from a *baguette* with some butter and preserves was jealously guarded as Madame's prerogative alone.

'Honestly,' Marty thought as she trailed after her towards what was presumably the kitchen, 'what a fuss about a little bit of bread and jam!'

She half expected to have it thrown at her, but instead she found herself in a large room, gleaming with the latest in kitchen equipment, with an immaculately clean scrubbed wooden table at which she was curtly invited to seat herself. Within minutes, bread miraculously still warm, and *croissants* were set set in front of her, together with a large slab of butter and a pot of home-made currant jam. Offered the choice, she picked chocolate in preference to coffee, and was served it in a big bowl with cream floating on top. Even the crumbs, and the last few drops lingering in the bottom of the bowl, tasted delectable.

'It was delicious,' she thanked Madame shyly when she had finished, but the overture received no response.

And now what? she asked herself, as she left the kitchen and wandered slowly back into the hall. There was no sign of Bernard, nor of his father. In fact the whole house had a curiously deserted air. Apart from that of the *salon* which stood ajar, the closed doors round the hall stared back at her with blank unwelcoming faces.

For a moment she hesitated, then she marched to the front door, and flinging it wide went out into the sunshine.

There was still a faint early chill in the air, and Marty clasped her arms in front of herself with a slight shiver. She stood irresolutely for a moment, wondering which direction to take. A stroll along the beach while it was still uncrowded seemed appealing, but the clustering pine trees offered a more immediate challenge, and she walked away from the house towards one of the tracks leading through the tall trunks. As she moved into the shadow of the trees, she had the oddest sensation that she was being watched, and she swung round, shading her eyes and staring back at the house. But there was no one in sight, no tell-tale flicker of movement at any of the unshuttered windows, merely the far-off whine of Madame's vacuum cleaner once more in operation.

'Imagination,' Marty muttered, and turned to continue her walk. A cry rose unuttered in her throat as one of the shadows detached itself and came forward. It was the dog César. Marty braced herself, then saw with astonishment that his tail was moving slowly. At least his hostility seemed to have waned during the night, even if no one else's had. She stretched out a tentative hand and with the air of one conferring a favour, he allowed her to stroke his head and fondle his ears. And when she moved off again down the track he padded gravely beside her, as if he was making her free of his domain. As indeed he probably was, she decided, and was more than glad he had not chosen to bar her from it instead.

'I don't know where we're going,' she told him frankly after a few minutes. 'I hope that you do.'

And it seemed that he did, for he bounded ahead of her with a little impetuous bark and vanished round the next bend. A moment later Marty heard him whining softly and quickened her own steps in sudden alarm. Had he been hurt? Could there be traps in these peaceful-looking woods? But when she rounded the corner, understanding came and the inevitable return of the previous night's sorrow. She found herself in a small clearing, in the centre of which was a fenced-off plot. It hardly needed the simple stone cross, with its brief inscription 'Jacques Langton' and a date to tell her that this was Uncle Jim's grave. César had gone to lie beside it, his head buried on his paws and as she approached he looked up and whined again.

'Poor old boy.' Marty came and squatted beside him, her fingers caressing the ruff of hair round his neck. 'Were you Uncle Jim's dog really? Did you go with the house?'

She felt the sting of tears against her eyelids as she spoke. It explained why César had accompanied her so readily. Perhaps he kept vigil here every day when he wasn't needed to scare the life out of unwanted visitors by his new master. Yet César wasn't the only one who came to the lonely grave in the pine forest, she realised as her eyes fell on the fresh-looking sheaf of gladioli which someone had placed there. She reached out and touched one of the peach-coloured blooms gently with the tips of her fingers.

'I'm glad you're not forgotten, Uncle Jim,' she whispered.

It was very quiet in the clearing, then a twig snapped somewhere nearby and César lifted his head and growled softly. Marty remained where she was very still, her mouth suddenly dry. It had just occurred to her how far from the house she probably was, and she had told no one where she was going before she set out, or even asked whether the woods were safe. And as every horror story she had ever heard or read about quiet and lonely places began to unfold like ancient newsreels across her mind, she felt César's muscles bunch under her hand as he lifted himself to his feet and bounded away from her. She wanted to call him back, but her throat wouldn't utter the sound, and she made herself get to her feet very slowly and turn.

As she did so, she heard César give a low ecstatic bark, and saw him leap up joyously at the man who had just emerged into the clearing.

'You!' Marty managed.

Luc Dumarais lifted a careless eyebrow as he bent to caress César's head.

'You were expecting someone else?'

'I wasn't expecting anyone at all,' she said. Her heart was thudding rapidly, but that was due to the shock of his unexpected appearance. 'I wasn't expecting to be followed, either,' she added defiantly.

He strolled forward. 'So you are one of the new breed of women who says that she can take care of herself on all occasions?'

'I hardly imagine any harm will come to me here,' she protested, interlacing her fingers nervously.

'Then it would be better if you stopped trusting your imagination, *ma petite*,' he said drily. 'You don't even know the extent of the forest. Didn't it occur to you that you could have become lost?'

She shrugged. 'It isn't exactly the sort of weather for dying of exposure.'

'Perhaps not.' His firm lips thinned. 'But there are other sorts of death to be included in the reckoning in a place as lonely as this. The death, *peut-être*, of an innocence even as stubborn and determined as yours seems to be.'

It would have been so easy then to agree, to confess her own misgivings, but some demon wouldn't allow her to do so—a demon that urged she should resent the implication that she was a naïve irresponsible child, who couldn't even be trusted to take a morning stroll on her own.

'But didn't you warn me yourself, *monsieur*, that appearances could be misleading. Perhaps I'm not the innocent you think me.'

His smile mocked her. 'Don't fling down any gauntlets to me, *chérie*,' he said unpleasantly. 'You would have far more to regret than I if I chose to accept your challenge, believe me. Besides, this is hardly the time or the place for us to conduct such a debate—or had you forgotten?'

Hot colour stole up into her cheeks and she folded her arms defensively across her breasts.

'I haven't forgotten anything,' she said after a moment's pause.

'I did not merely follow you as a safety precaution,' he went on. 'When I saw the direction you had taken I knew what you would find, and I thought you might require an explanation.'

'An explanation?'

'Why Jacques should be buried here, and not in consecrated ground.'

'I see.' She spread her hands rather falteringly. 'To be frank it never occurred to me. It all seemed—so right, somehow.'

He nodded. 'It is good that you feel that way. It was what Jacques himself wanted—to be buried among the pines, within the sound of the sea.'

'And the flowers?' She gestured towards the grave. 'Who brought the flowers?'

He gave a slight shrug. 'He had many friends. Is it important for you to know the exact identity?'

'No,' she said with a little sigh. 'Are these—the gladioli —what Uncle Jim tried to grow on his farm?'

'No. He grew tulips—this region is famous for them. But there were difficulties. His first season was a bad one— he did not know the markets.' He shook his head. 'Maybe if he had been a younger man, in better health, he might have learned from his mistakes. But he wanted too much too soon. He wanted to make money quickly.'

'I don't need to ask why,' she said drearily.

'No, I don't suppose that you do. Nor why he did not wish you to know of his failure. He was a proud man. He set his own standards and lived by them. This time he drove himself too hard.'

'Yes.' Marty gave the grave a last look, then turned away. As she walked back towards the track, she caught her foot against a stone and stumbled slightly. Instantly his hand was beneath her elbow, steadying her.

'*Attention!*' he warned brusquely.

'I'm all right.' She pulled herself free with more haste than good manners, and saw his eyes narrow unpleasantly.

'What are you frightened of?' he drawled. 'That my animal lusts are going to overwhelm me? You flatter yourself, Martine. Must I warn you again about trusting your imagination?'

Her face flamed. 'You're very insulting,' she defended herself feebly.

'You consider it an insult because a man does not try to make love to you?'

'No! You're twisting everything I say,' she retorted heatedly. 'It—it's an insult to imply that I spend my life waiting for you to—pounce on me.'

'Such a thought, of course, has never crossed your virginal mind.'

'No, it hasn't.' She met his sardonic gaze, chin lifted in defiance.

'I am delighted to hear it.' His eyes left hers and moved down to rest for a significant moment on her parted, quivering lips, the tell-tale pulse throbbing in her throat, the uneven rise and fall of her breasts. 'You seem curiously disturbed, *ma mie*. If this is how you react to a hand on your arm, then what would you do if you were kissed, I wonder?'

There was something in his tone that flicked her on the raw—a faint amusement as if he knew how many first times were being covered in his teasing. Knew that she had never been held in a man's arms, or felt his body close to hers and his mouth closing upon her own.

'That need hardly concern you, *monsieur*,' she said tightly. 'Now, if you'll let me pass, I'll go back to the house.'

He moved his shoulders lazily inside the thin black high-necked sweater he was wearing.

'Run away if you must,' he said mockingly. 'But you surely don't imagine that I followed you here simply to protect you from lurking rapists or assassins?'

'I no longer trust my imagination, *monsieur*.' She spoke with a calmness she was far from feeling. 'Remember?'

'Bravo!' He was laughing at her openly now. 'You learn fast, Martine. I think the next lesson must be how not to rise quite so quickly to the bait.' His eyes returned smilingly to her mouth. 'Unless you would prefer a different kind of lesson entirely.'

'I think I've learned enough for one morning,' she said, forcing her tone to lightness and returning his smile. 'But I'll bear your offer in mind, *monsieur*.'

'And my other offer? When you left the villa this morning without a word to anyone, it occurred to me that you might have decided on some reckless course of action—like running away.'

'So that was why you came after me?'

'*Naturellement.*' His mouth twisted. 'I hope you are not too disappointed.'

'Now I think you're flattering yourself, *monsieur*,' she returned with all the coolness she could have desired. 'No, I'm not disappointed. Nor am I given to reckless acts. I was just going for a stroll—not running away.'

'I am grateful for your assurances—on all counts,' he said drily. 'But do you honestly believe that coming here at all, without checking, without making certain that the offer you had received was genuine was not a reckless act?'

'It didn't seem so,' she said tiredly. 'I'd been expecting it for so long, you see. When the letter came it was like the answer to a prayer.'

'Oh, all our prayers are answered, *ma mie*,' he said sardonically. 'But not always in the manner that we expect. Last night I put certain propositions to you. Now I need an answer. Do you go or stay?'

The silence began to lengthen, to become endless. Marty stood staring down at the rough ground. She knew what she ought to answer, knew it immediately. The sensible, the correct thing to do was to get away from here now, before it was too late. But too late for what? She didn't even know. She had been told not to trust her imagination. Should she trust her instincts?

'I am waiting, Martine,' his voice reminded her levelly at last.

She moistened her dry lips desperately. I must go, she thought. I must get away from here. No one really wants me to stay—not Bernard, nor Madame Guisard, and certainly not this man who disturbs me more than anyone I have ever met. All I ever wanted was to be safe, and what safety is there, sharing a house with a man who attracts me and frightens me at one and the same time? And if he ever touched me—really touched me, I think I would break into a million little pieces.

A breeze like a sigh whispered through the pines, and somewhere quite near at hand a bird began to sing, a brilliant carillon of sound that seemed to go on and on.

She lifted a hand and smoothed back the hair which the breeze had ruffled.

'I'd like to stay,' she said.

'*Bon.*' His nod seemed to indicate that her acquiescence was no more than he had expected, but gave no sign whether he was pleased or otherwise by her decision. 'Naturally I should not expect you to start work immediately. Take a few days—get to know the house, the beach— get to know Bernard, if he'll let you,' he added cynically. 'Then we'll talk again.'

'Yes,' she said tonelessly. Then, as he turned away along the track, 'Thank you, *monsieur*. I'm very grateful.'

'What an effort that must have cost,' he said mockingly. 'And don't be too prodigal with your gratitude, Martine, until you find out exactly what is required of you.'

His long lithe stride carried him away from her down the track, and at the bend he did not even bother to turn back to see if she was following. Which, of course, she was. At a safe distance, she told herself ironically.

The problem was—with a man like Luc Dumarais, what distance was ever going to be completely safe for her?

Whatever good intentions Marty might have had were destined to be unfulfilled. When they arrived back at the villa, Madame Guisard was waiting with a thunderous expression. She did not glance at Marty, but burst at once into a torrent of complaint and recrimination in her own language directed at Luc Dumarais. Glancing down at him, Marty saw his dark brows drawing together in a frown.

Eventually he dismissed Madame with a quiet word, and she returned presumably to her kitchen, muttering under her breath.

'Is something the matter?' Marty asked.

Luc shrugged. 'It's Bernard.' His voice sounded cool and remote. 'It seems he has stolen some food from the larder, and taken himself off for the day.' He saw the anxious expression which crossed her face, and his voice softened almost imperceptibly. 'Don't blame yourself, Martine. This is not the first time he has done this, believe me. I only wish it could be the last.'

'Where does he go?'

He spread his hand. 'To the beach, *sans doute*. I don't blame him for that. But it makes me angry when he consults no one—fails to even mention his plans for the day. And his behaviour over the food upsets Albertine.'

Marty remained silent. She had no idea what to reply. The episode seemed to demonstrate just how wide the gulf was between Bernard and his father, and in spite of Luc Dumarais' reassurance, she could not help thinking it was significant that Bernard had chosen this particular morning for another assertion of his independence.

And she had actually thought as they walked back to the house that perhaps the fact that Bernard had sought her out earlier, albeit to warn her against staying, might be a hopeful sign. It was obvious now that he was indifferent to whether she stayed or went, and although it was foolish to feel hurt, she had to admit to a slightly wounded feeling. She was, she knew, being totally illogical. She had already resigned herself to the fact that no one at Solitaire really desired her presence, but she would have to harden herself against that. She had to earn money before she could leave, and part of that money would be earned by providing companionship for Bernard, although it would not be easy forcing her company on someone who had shown so clearly that it was unwanted.

Meanwhile, she was now at a loose end. Luc Dumarais had already said that her secretarial duties could wait for a few days, and now that Bernard had vanished she had nothing to do. She could, she supposed with a little supressed sigh, go and rearrange the sparse contents of her drawers and wardrobe, but that wouldn't take very long. She wandered across the hall towards the stairs, but as she set her foot on the bottom step, Luc's voice arrested her.

'Where are you going?' He was standing in the doorway of the *salon* watching her.

'Up to my room,' she replied briefly.

'Why don't you go to the beach?'

'To find Bernard?' She wrinkled her forehead.

He smiled without humour. 'I doubt you could do that— unless Bernard wished to be found. He can be most elusive when he wishes. No, I suggested the beach for your own amusement. You like to lie in the sun, don't you—to swim?'

'I suppose so,' she said guardedly. Aunt Mary, she recalled, had never had any time for the sheer idleness of sunbathing. And while Marty had been taught the rudiments of swimming at school, her young life had never been enlivened by trips to the seaside.

His eyes narrowed. 'You do swim?'

'A little.'

'How little?' he demanded brusquely. 'You must realise that this is the Atlantic coast. The sea is often quite rough, and there is a strong undertow. Perhaps you had better wait to swim until someone can go with you for the first time. But you could go on the sand for a while, as long as you don't allow yourself to get burned.'

'And take my bucket and spade, no doubt.' Sudden temper possessed Marty. 'Thank you, Monsieur Dumarais, but I'm really not quite that much of a child. And I have seen the sun before. Oddly enough we do have summers in England—quite hot ones sometimes.'

'How very patriotic of you.' He sounded almost amused. 'But my warning still stands, *ma mie*. The warmth of our sun is like passion, not to be underestimated until it has been fully experienced.' He paused mockingly. 'But perhaps since you insist you are not a child, you have ex-

perienced that too?' There was derision in the glance he
sent her, but there was something else as well—a new
element which invaded her fragile defences as if they did
not exist, and brought a swift tormented flush to her
cheeks.

'No, I thought not,' he said sardonically after a pause
in which Marty had been trying frantically to think of
a remark—witty, poised and sophisticated—which would
totally demolish him. 'It's cruel to tease you, isn't it, *ma
belle*—like robbing an infant of its sweets. Go and enjoy
your day on the beach. *Un coup de soleil* is probably a
safer experience than *un coup d'amour* at this stage in
your life.'

'I don't want to go to the beach.' Marty pushed de-
featedly at the strand of chestnut hair which insisted on
falling across her cheek. 'I—I think I'll go up to my room.'

'In glorious weather like this?' He raised his eyebrows.
'Are you mad?'

'I haven't got a swimming costume,' Marty said baldly,
goaded into the admission. She had outgrown the school
regulation costume years before, and buying a replace-
ment under the circumstances had seemed pointless, as well
as an unnecessary extravagance. And until that moment she
had not fully absorbed the implications of coming to live
near the sea. It was the thought of having a home of her
own at last that brought her here, not the actual environ-
men.

Luc Dumarais raised his eyebrows. 'That isn't an in-
soluble problem. There are shops in Les Sables des Pins
which sell little else.' He glanced at his wristwatch. 'Or if
you need a wider selection, you may come with me to La
Rochelle. I have business there this morning.'

He saw her obvious hesitation, and a look of irritation
crossed his dark face.

'What is the matter now?'

Marty swallowed. She had gained a fair idea on her
journey through France of the gulf that yawned between

British and Continental prices.

'I was just—wondering about the cost,' she began lamely, and could have bitten her tongue out. Luc Dumarais might be behaving like King Cophetua, but she was damned if she was going to play the beggarmaid.

'Don't let it concern you.' He sounded amused again. 'It will be my pleasure . . .'

'Well, it won't be mine,' she said frankly. 'I wasn't hinting that you should buy me a swimming costume, although it may have sounded like that, and I certainly couldn't accept such a gift from——' she had been going to say 'a man' but she realised how prudish and old-fashioned it sounded and was reluctant to expose herself to his mockery yet again, so she substituted 'anyone' instead.

He looked faintly surprised. 'Calm yourself, *ma mie*. I have no intention of buying your clothes for you. What I had intended to offer was an advance on your salary, or will your pride not permit you to accept that either?'

Marty groaned inwardly. Once again it seemed he had succeeded in putting her in the wrong, and it would have been wonderful to have told him precisely what he could do with his salary advance, and his job for that matter, and stormed out of the house and out of his life for ever. One day she would, she promised herself. Oh, she would tell him, in English and in French to ensure there was no chance of any misunderstanding. And in the meantime, she would see just as little of him as was humanly possible.

'And don't refuse to come to La Rochelle with me,' he said, diagnosing the trend of her thoughts with uncanny accuracy. 'It's a beautiful town, and very old. And it's part of your history as well as ours.'

But it wasn't history that concerned her, she thought almost hysterically. It was the immediate future. She didn't think she could cope with the strain of a morning in his company in spite of the lure of shops and ancient buildings —an almost irresistible combination. But for the sake of her own peace of mind, she had to resist. Any excuse would do, even a lame one. The last thing Luc Dumarais would be used to would be having his invitations turned down, and if she refused him once, she was certain he would never ask her again. It was a simple solution and a certain one. All she had to do was speak.

Incredulously she heard a voice she hardly recognised as belonging to her saying, 'Thank you, *monsieur*. I—I'll go and change.'

'As you please.' He lit a cigarette. 'I'll have the car at the front of the house in'—he consulted his watch again—'fifteen minutes. Will that give you enough time?'

She agreed rather faintly, and went away from him up the stairs. Her pulses were pounding, and she felt a curious sense of unreality which even the smooth curve of the balustrade rail under her fingers could not dispel. When she gained her room, she closed the door and leaned against it for a moment, her eyes staring ahead of her unseeingly.

'Oh God,' she whispered at last. 'What am I doing? What's happening to me?'

She rinsed her hands and face, before applying a trace of make-up to her eyes and lips, and putting on her only new dress—a cream, full-skirted affair with a bold Mexican border print.

When she looked at herself in the mirror, it was like seeing a stranger standing there—a stranger whose parted lips were soft and vulnerable, and whose eyes glowed with an unrecognisable excitement. A stranger who whispered aloud 'Fool!' before she turned away on a long, shaking breath and went out of the room and down the stairs to where Luc Dumarais was waiting for her.

CHAPTER FIVE

THE drive to La Rochelle took just under an hour. Marty had been perfectly correct in her supposition that Luc's choice of car would not be one of the small economical models. She didn't know much about cars, so she was not prepared to hazard a guess as to what make the sleek silver-grey monster she found herself in was, but she could recognise power when she saw it and she was forced to admire Luc's almost nonchalant handling of that power.

Their route was a fairly tortuous one, at one moment running along the coast, at the next turning inland into narrow-streeted towns which, over the years, had yielded little to the demands of the motor car.

Luc spoke little, and when he did, it was merely to point out some landmark or stretch of scenery. Marty was thankful for that. She found it difficult to believe that she was actually sitting in the car beside him and still did not fully understand what had prompted her to agree to make the trip in his company. None of the answers which had suggested themselves while she was changing had been of any consolation whatsoever.

It was quite simple, she tried to tell herself. She was merely over-reacting to an attractive man, and perhaps a few hours spent in close proximity to him might put her well on the way to being cured. Or at least familiarity would reduce the intensity of this awareness she experienced every time he came near her—wouldn't it? Marty wasn't sure. In fact she wasn't sure of anything, except that by deciding to stay in France she had only added to the difficulties of her ultimate and inevitable departure.

Yet she could not be too unhappy in spite of everything. It was a glorious day, bakingly warm although the sun had

77

not yet reached its full height, and Marty was grateful for the faint breeze coming in through the car's open windows. Almost before she realised it they were on the broad carriageway which took them through the outskirts of La Rochelle. Luc took the turning to the town centre, and parked in an enormous car park in a large square near the cathedral.

Marty picked up her handbag and prepared to get out of the car, but he detained her.

'Aren't you forgetting something?' he asked, and held out an envelope.

She hesitated. 'It really isn't necessary,' she began, totally untruthfully.

He sighed. 'Take the money, Martine,' he advised brusquely. 'I promise you that you will earn it, if that makes you feel any better about the transaction.'

'Thank you,' she mumbled, stowing the envelope inside her bag.

'*Bon.*' He flicked at her cheek with a careless finger. 'And be careful of pickpockets, *hein*? It's early in the season, so they'll be on the look-out for little tourists.'

He swung his long legs out of the car and secured the door, before coming round and opening her door.

Marty looked at her watch. 'What time do you want me to come back here?' she enquired diffidently.

He paused in the act of checking that her door was locked and raised an interrogative eyebrow. 'It that a pointed hint to me that you want to be alone? *Quel dommage*. I thought we would meet for *déjeuner.*'

'I shall be quite all right,' she assured him quickly. 'I thought you said you had business to attend to.'

'I have, but it will not take me all day.' His dark eyes studied her frowningly. 'Nor will your shopping occupy the whole of your time. However, if you don't wish to have lunch with me ...' He lifted a dismissive shoulder, and pocketed his car keys.

Marty bit her lip. 'It's not a question of that,' she began

haltingly. 'I—I just don't want to get in the way.'

His glance was quizzical, but not unfriendly. 'Don't worry, *ma mie*,' he said lightly. 'I would not permit that. I'll take you to the Syndicat now and get you a street map, and we'll arrange a place to meet and a time.'

And there was a warning, if ever there was one, Marty thought miserably as she followed his tall figure across the square and down a side-street where buildings whose upper storeys overhung the pavements and graceful stone arches provided some welcome shade from the all-pervasive sun.

The Syndicat d'Initiative was soon reached. Although it was still early in the season, there were already a number of people there, buying local guides as well as more regional literature, and the clerks on the tall counter were kept busy finding accommodation for those who were touring in the area.

Marty watched Luc Dumarais push through the throng of people to the counter and return after a minute with a small guide book in his hand.

There was a street map inside it, and when they were outside again he showed her their exact location, and the best way to reach the market and the Hotel de Ville as well as other places of interest.

'I won't presume to tell you where to find the shops,' he said with a faint smile. 'I imagine like most women you could find them even if your eyes were blindfolded.'

Marty returned the smile, but remained silent. There was little point in protesting how few and far between such expeditions had been in her life. It would be of no interest to him, even if he believed her.

'*Alors.*' He glanced at his watch. 'I will leave you now as I have an appointment. But we'll meet at noon on this corner'—his finger stabbed a spot on the map—'and find somewhere to eat.'

Marty was aware of an odd feeling of helplessness as she watched his tall figure stride up the street, and disappear round the corner. For most of her life, it seemed, she had been under someone's domination. First it had been Aunt Mary, and now, with even less justification it was Luc Dumarais. Aunt Mary's domination had been prompted, she thought, by a sense of reluctant responsibility, but Luc's was not nearly so easy to define. Presumably, as her employer, he assumed he had the right to give her orders, but she was not officially working for him yet. For a moment she tried to imagine Mr Leslie taking her to shop for a swimsuit, and then ordering her to have lunch with him, and a reluctant smile curved her lips.

In the meantime, she could stand here outside the Syndicat wondering about his motivation for the remainder of the morning, or she could begin her exploration of La Rochelle, and thrust all her doubts and questions to the back of her mind to be dealt with at a more appropriate time.

She spent an enchanted morning. She joined the other tourists in a guided trip round the Hotel de Ville, where she soon gave up the unequal struggle to understand the whole of the commentary, and contented herself with simply devoting her wholehearted appreciation to the relics of a bygone age which were on show there. When it was over, she wandered across to the pavement café opposite and took a seat under one of the umbrellas, rustling slightly in the faint breeze. She ordered a glass of lemon tea, and while the waiter was bringing her order, she glanced in the envelope that Luc had given her.

At first she didn't believe her eyes, then she began to feel sick, and a little angry. She had never had so much money in her possession before. No wonder he had told her to beware of pickpockets! She swallowed, and with unsteady fingers transferred some of the notes to an inside zipped pocket in her bag.

But how dared he! she thought. Her tea was placed in front of her, but her appetite for it had vanished completely. She paid the surprised waiter and got up and left, pushing her untouched glass to one side.

Marty turned into another street, giving no thought to her surroundings, or the route she was taking, the guide book neglected in her bag. An advance on her salary, he had said, she thought furiously. As far as she could judge, the sum he had given her would have covered her pay packet for several months in England. He wasn't merely giving her adequate remuneration for her services; he seemed to be buying her body and soul. Well, I won't be bought, she told herself, nor will I be treated as a charity case. Just who does he think he's trying to impress? He's already established the fact that he's wealthy and famous. He doesn't have to grind it in my teeth.

She found there were unexpected tears stinging at her eyelids. It was so easy, she thought, for the rich of the world, and so hard for those who merely wanted to enjoy an adequate living. Uncle Jim had lost everything because he wasn't sufficiently skilled in the art of making money. And Luc Dumarais had come along and taken it all from him—the house, the land, everything.

But not me, she whispered fiercely to herself. I'm not included in his package deal. The very thought made her writhe inwardly with humiliation. He might have everything else that Uncle Jim had once owned, but he would never have her.

She looked up and saw that she had emerged from the street on to a section of the harbour. The breeze was stronger here and full of salt, and she breathed deeply, filling her lungs with the clean invigorating air. The sun felt warm on her face as she moved forward, towards the bright water and its flotilla of bobbing craft. It was lively and noisy and colourful and perceptibly she felt her anger begin to ebb away and her spirits lift again as she stared across the sunlit water to the massive towers which guarded the old fort. She found herself a seat in the shade, and made herself think calmly and rationally about her best course of action. Her immediate impulse had been to seek out Luc Dumarais and indignantly fling his money back at him, but she knew that would be both rude and pointless. Instead she found a scrap of paper and a pen and rather laboriously worked out what a week of her former salary would be at the current exchange rate. Then she carefully counted the amount out from the wad of notes that Luc Dumarais had given her, and replaced the remainder back in the envelope, sealing it. The equivalent to her salary, she stowed away in her purse. It was, she discovered, depressingly little, recalling most of the prices she had seen in the shops, but it would have to do. After all, once her duties at Solitaire began in real earnest, her opportunities for shopping might be few and far between. And the very act of restricting herself to what she felt was her due entitlement made her feel infinitely more reconciled to the whole transaction.

She gave a little start of surprise as she glanced at her watch. She had not left herself a great deal of time for buying the swimsuit that Luc Dumarais had ordained. She hesitated for a moment, sorely tempted not to bother, then got to her feet with a sigh. It was probably better to obey him in this than suffer the inevitable recriminations. Besides, common sense told her that it would be enjoyable to go on the beach and enjoy the glorious weather, dressed, or undressed, in exactly the same way as everyone else.

She consulted her street map, and set off back towards the main shopping area. Normally she would have enjoyed a leisurely jaunt round the boutiques, comparing styles and prices, but time was running too short for that, so she went into the first boutique displaying beachwear in the window and asked in her best French to be shown some swimming costumes. She hesitated when it came to the Continental sizings, but in fact there was no need for her to worry as Madame who had come forward to serve her had already run a professional eye over her slender contours, and was already laying a selection on the counter for her to look at.

Marty picked them up and studied them, her eyes

widening. They were some of the briefest bikinis she had ever seen—most of them little more than tiny triangles of fabric held together by strings of the same colour. She had never worn anything like it in her life. Flushing slightly, she put them back on the counter, and asked Madame if she had anything with slightly more to it. Madame seemed a little surprised, but she quickly produced a new selection, and Marty realised with a sinking heart that she had made her think that she wanted a more expensive rather than a slightly more decent range. As it was, the price tickets on the first selection had made her eyes widen incredulously. They must charge by the square millimetre! she thought.

She shook her head and, thankful there was no one else in the shop at that precise moment, set out to show Madame with gestures as well as words precisely what she had in mind.

But Madame, it was soon clear, was not convinced by her arguments. What reason, she wanted to know, did Mademoiselle have for wishing to cover herself? For the young and slender, after all, all things were possible, and she urged Marty at least to try some of the bikinis on and see how well they became her.

It was difficult to maintain her position in the face of such flattering and persuasive tactics, but Marty remained adamant. Mendaciously, she invented an elderly aunt who would be deeply offended by such exposure. Madame's deep answering shrug indicated scepticism of anyone, however stricken in years, who took such an unrealistic view of life, but in response to Marty's plea, she went away and came back with some one-piece swimsuits over her arm.

Once again the prices were enough to set Marty's head reeling. Even the cheapest, she realised, would make an unholy rent in the advance she had reserved. Perhaps Luc Dumarais had been neither devious nor patronising, but simply realistic when he had given her all that money, she thought unhappily. However, she had already decided what she was going to do about that, and she would not go back on her decision, however tempting it might be.

Quietly, and to Madame's evident disappointment, she picked the plainest and cheapest of the suits. It fitted her well, she told herself as she gazed at her reflection in the mirror of the small changing cubicle, and the dark green colour was quite becoming with her chestnut hair and pale skin.

She handed over the money to Madame who accepted it with another fatalistic shrug, and went out carrying her small striped carrier. It was time now for her rendezvous with Luc Dumarais. She knew she ought to hurry, but involuntarily her footsteps began to slow. Some time during lunch, or just after, she would have to return that money to him, and there was every chance that he would be very angry. He was not, after all, a man who liked to have his will crossed, she thought apprehensively. All she could do was explain that she would never have accepted a *centime* piece from him, if she had realised how much the envelope contained, and weather the only too probable storm that would follow.

She gave a little sigh. It would be much easier to avoid the whole issue for a while by pretending she had forgotten where to meet him. She could use the time instead to look round some of the entrancing shops she had perforce to pass by—bookshops—leather, antiques, perfumes, and even art galleries, their sense of period emphasised by the overhanging buildings and the cobbled streets.

Above the chatter, the footsteps and the distant hum of the traffic, she could hear the tones of violin and accordion where a pair of street musicians played in one of the arcades, and she dropped a few coins into the hat placed hopefully on the ground beside them.

There was some intriguing smells to encounter along the way. As well as the sensuous allure of the numerous *parfumiers*, there was the mouthwatering aroma of freshly cooked waffles and *crêpes*, bringing home to Marty just how hungry she was. And further on, from the doorway of a large sweetshop, a beguiling smell of hot caramel. She had resisted the waffles, but this she could not resist, so she went in. At the back of the shop she could see the work tables where the mounds of caramel and other mixtures were being kneaded and stirred. Elsewhere, trays of finished sweets were being given the final trimmings and decorations by white-overalled women.

If you had time enough to spare, Marty thought, you could see the whole process from first to last, but as she had to hurry away, she would content herself by buying a few samples from the well-stocked shelves. She would keep them, she thought, as a souvenir of her day in La Rochelle, for there was no one back in England who would expect a present from her. She browsed happily for a few moments before selecting a round box of candies in the shape of sea shells, and a tall cellophane container filled to the brim with a delectable dark red confection, studded with nuts and smelling of liqueur. By the time she had waited for her purchases to be meticulously packaged and beribboned, she knew she was going to be late for her appointment.

She hurried along, dodging around groups of lunchtime saunterers, but resisting the impulse to break into a run. Late she might be, but at least she wouldn't be hot, breathless and late. Besides, she crossed her fingers at her side, Luc might have been held up himself. She might be there ahead of him.

But that was too much to hope for, she soon realised, as she cut through the market place, now almost deserted, and saw his tall figure pacing up and down on the corner he had indicated. She saw him glance at his watch, and his frown, although he had not seen her, seemed to reach out and grip her by the throat, making her swallow nervously.

Don't be a fool, she adjured herself robustly. You're only a few minutes late. He can't eat you.

She slowed her steps deliberately to a casual amble, swinging the carrier she held as if she had all the time in the world as she went up to him. She was still a few feet away when he swung round and saw her.

One long, furious stride brought him right up to her, his hand gripping her arm.

'Where in the name of God have you been?' he demanded tersely.

Marty shrugged. 'Shopping,' she returned vaguely. 'Have —have you been waiting long?'

'Long enough,' he said grimly. 'Long enough to be worried—to wonder whether you had become lost, or were in some other kind of trouble.'

'Or whether I'd run away?' she countered.

'No.' His eyes narrowed. 'Frankly that was not a possibility that occurred to me. But La Rochelle is a port, and no doubt has its share of unsavoury characters like most ports. You could have been abducted—or robbed.'

Which was, she supposed, as good as opening as any. 'Monsieur,' she began, 'about the money you advanced to me . . .'

'Have you lost it?' He slanted a look at her.

'Certainly not!' she denied indignantly. 'But I must talk to you about it.'

'Later,' he said briefly. The punishing grip left her arm, and he slid a hand beneath her elbow urging her forward. 'After we've eaten.'

And there was no arguing with that, Marty told herself resignedly, as she had to almost break into a trot to keep up with his long stride. Never come between a Frenchman and his food.

The restaurant she eventually stopped outside in a side street was not particularly prepossessing in appearance. The interior was slightly Spartan too—hard wooden chairs and benches, and businesslike tables covered with white cloths and laid with the bare minimum of knives, forks and wine glasses. But, Marty noticed, nearly all the tables were occupied, and the proprietor, a slight man whose heavy, rather lugubrious moustache was belied by the twinkle in his dark eyes, was scurrying backwards and forwards to the big stone-flagged kitchen at the back of the restaurant, transmitting orders and conveying first courses to the diners, most of whom seemed to be awaiting his advent with some impatience, their table napkins tucked into their collars.

Luc Dumarais put Marty into a seat at a corner table and passed her the handwritten menu.

'Do you need me to translate for you?' he enquired.

'I can manage,' she averred with dignity. But it wasn't the easiest of tasks. As usual there were a number of menus on the card at differing prices, each one incorporating at least two choices of dish for each course. She found she was looking from one to another and back again, but coming no closer to making up her mind.

'Make haste, Martine,' her companion suggested lazily after a while. 'You are making Philippe quite anxious. In a moment or two he will think that nothing that he and Madame have devised appeal to you, and you'll take the English way out and order an omelette.'

'It isn't that.' She peered at the card with increasing desperation. 'I just can't make up my mind.'

Luc Dumarais sighed deeply and said something to the hovering *patron* in a low voice which made him shout with laughter, and return his own delighted comment on '*les femmes*' and their vagaries.

Luc turned back to her. 'Will you allow me to choose for us both?'

'That would probably be best,' she agreed meekly, and handed back the card. The order was taken, a carafe of wine was brought and a basket of bread, cut into hearty chunks.

Luc Dumarais poured some wine into each glass, and then leaned back in his chair.

'Was your shopping expedition a success?' he asked.

'Yes, thank you,' she returned rather primly. She cleared her throat. 'About the money, *monsieur* ...'

'I did say after we'd eaten,' he reminded her. He picked up his glass and studied the wine.

Marty subsided, feeling snubbed. Which was probably exactly how he intended her to feel, she thought bitterly. That was almost certainly the lordly way in which he usually dismissed unwanted topics of conversation. Well, in this case she was just as determined as he was!

Her attention was diverted, however, by the return of the *patron* carrying a serving platter and two plates. Marty gasped aloud when she saw what the platter contained.

'Oysters?'

'Oysters,' Luc Dumarais confirmed in a tone of total unconcern, shaking out his table napkin. 'Don't you like them?'

'I've never had them,' she said. 'As you're probably quite well aware.'

'Then it will be a new experience for you.' Was there a hint of unholy amusement under his level voice? He spooned some of the oysters on her plate and added a chunk of fresh lemon, before passing her a small silver fork.

'*Voilà*,' he said. 'A squeeze of lemon juice, and then you remove them from their shells—so.' He demonstrated with practised ease.

'What do you do then?' Marty asked weakly.

'Most people eat them.' This time he made no attempt to hide his amusement.

'Are you supposed to swallow them whole?' She bit her lip. 'Because I don't think I ...'

He interrupted her, shaking his head. 'No, no, Martine. You eat them in the way that seems most comfortable to you. If you wish to chew them, then do so. *Allons*,' he nodded encouragingly towards her plate.

She took a deep breath, then picked up a wedge of lemon. The oyster, apparently resigned to its fate, was detached from the shell without difficulty and she raised the succulent morsel to her lips apprehensively.

Luc Dumarais paused to watch her, and saw the anxious expression in her eyes turn to a look of sheer wonder.

'But it's beautiful!' she exclaimed. 'It's like eating the sun and the sea together.'

'I'm glad that you approve,' he said blandly. 'It would have been a tragedy if anyone so young and lovely had refused the food of love.'

Marty put down her fork. 'The food of love?' she said in a hollow voice.

'But yes.' He scooped out another oyster and ate it with undisguised relish, his dark eyes mocking her. 'From the earliest times they have been recognised as a potent aphrodisiac. Didn't you know?'

'No,' Marty said stonily, 'I didn't.'

His smile widened. Before she could stop him, he picked up the platter and served some more on to her plate.

'*Bon appetit*,' he said sardonically. 'Don't look so panic-stricken, *chérie*. I am not about to test the truth of their power—at least, not here. You are quite safe to finish your meal.'

She flushed scarlet, angry with him and also with herself for rising so easily to his baiting. She had been sorely tempted to push her plate away, leaving the delectable remainder of her oysters untouched, but she knew that the effect of any such action would be to make her look even more foolish, as well as depriving her of the oysters. So, giving him a fulminating glance, she picked up her fork again.

The next course proved to be a savoury home-made terrine, cut into thick slices and nestling in a bed of green salad.

Before she started on her portion, Marty sent Luc Dumarais a dulcet smile.

'Are there any interesting legends about this as well which I should know before I begin?' she asked sweetly.

'I don't think so.' He pretended to consider. 'I think the people of La Rochelle probably utter a prayer of thankfulness each time it's brought to the table that they're not still living on siege rations, but that is all.'

'Siege rations?' she queried.

'But yes.' He nodded. 'In the days of the wars of religion

in France, La Rochelle was a rich and independent community, and perhaps because of this, it opted for the Huguenot cause. It was besieged twice by the Catholic forces. The first time it withstood the siege, but the second time, in 1628, things did not go quite so well. They depended, *vous savez*, on a relieving force from England coming to their rescue, so they starved, hoping that this help would come.' He glanced across at her. 'You didn't know this from your schooldays—from your history lessons?'

'Our history lessons weren't awfully interesting,' she admitted. 'We always seemed to go straight from the Middle Ages to the Industrial Revolution. We missed out on the really romantic periods.'

He shrugged. 'I doubt whether those who survived the famine saw themselves as figures of romance, although there was great heroism, *sans doute*. They ate dogs and rats, and even pieces of leather soaked in water. Terrible disease broke out as a result.' He paused. 'Didn't you see the plaque in the market place?'

'No,' she admitted. 'So what happened in the end?'

'The English fleet went home—and La Rochelle surrendered to Richelieu. In a way—because of the sufferings of the people—it has always seemed to me more of a victory than a defeat.'

Marty looked at him rather shyly, aware of the depth of feeling with which he had spoken. 'Have you never considered making a film on the subject?'

'At one time, yes,' he said slowly. 'But I came to see that what concerns people is not the past, but the future. Besides, such a film would require an enormous budget and I do not always have that amount of finance at my disposal. So I concentrate on the present day and its problems.'

'That's rather a pity,' she said thoughtfully. 'I think it would make a marvellous film.'

His lip curled slightly. 'On the lines of the Hollywood epic?' he enquired. 'All the women in low-cut bodices, and a fantasy hero duelling to the death with Richelieu on the battlements?'

'No,' she protested. 'It doesn't have to be like that at all. I saw a play in England once about a village in Derbyshire which got the plague in the seventeenth century and deliberately cut itself off from all outside contact so that the disease didn't spread. Most of them died as well. Now that wasn't sensationalised in any way, but I've never forgotten it. One of the girls had a sweetheart in the next village and when he came for her at the end, he found she had died too.'

He raised his eyebrows. 'So what shall we give our heroine?' he asked. 'A lover in the English fleet?'

'You're laughing at me again,' she said in a subdued voice.

'I beg your pardon.' Unexpectedly he reached across the table and took her hand. The gesture startled her, and her heart began to thud slowly and painfully. She wanted to draw her hand away, and yet in another way she wanted the moment to last for ever. 'A film of the siege, made seriously, as you suggest, has been a dream of mine for years, but I have found so few people to share the dream with me that I have become cynical on the subject.'

'It's a pity to become cynical about dreams,' Marty said quietly. Any second now, she thought breathlessly, and he would hear the sound of her heart loud and unsteady in the stillness that seemed to encompass them in the middle of the crowded restaurant.

'Apply your wisdom to yourself, *ma mie*.' He smiled faintly. 'It is too late for me.'

'But you're not old,' she said impetuously, and could have bitten her tongue in half.

He laughed. '*Merci du compliment, mademoiselle.* Yet I have forgotten what it was like to be your age, and look with innocence on the world spread out before me.' The dark face was suddenly harsh as it studied hers, and he withdrew his hand almost roughly. 'I hope your ultimate awakening is gentler than mine was,' he added, and she wondered if he was thinking about his broken marriage, and the hostility of the only child who shared his solitude in the pine forest.

It was almost a relief when the *patron* came bustling up with a large dish almost overflowing with chicken and mushrooms in a thin delectable gravy, accompanied by a bowl of white haricot beans and a dressing of fresh tomatoes. The arrival of the food changed the mood completely, and Marty told herself she ought to be glad of this. For a brief while the atmosphere had been charged with a strange intimacy, and she didn't want that. For one thing there was no future in it. When her money was earned she was going back to England and that was all there was to it, and while she could not deny the attraction of Luc Dumarais' potent virility—and when he set out to be charming, she thought, he was almost irresistible—that attraction was purely a one-way process. And a picture of the dark sophisticated beauty she had seen him with only the previous evening rose vividly in her mind.

Food, she thought detachedly, as the chicken fell off its bones and melted ecstatically in her mouth, was a great consolation, and the French, she had to admit, were far more practical about such matters than the English. She only hoped that she could retain her own streak of practicality in the weeks ahead.

By the time she laid her knife and fork down, she felt ready for anything.

'Some fruit to follow?' Luc Dumarais picked up his wine glass and drained it.

Marty shook her head. 'I couldn't eat another thing.' She sighed. 'I wonder what was in that sauce?'

'I daresay Clotilde would tell you.' He sounded amused. 'Do you want me to ask her?'

'Certainly not,' she said hastily.

As the smiling *patron* arrived at their table to take the order for coffee, she was embarrassed to hear Luc Dumarais say lazily, 'Mademoiselle wishes to congratulate you, Philippe, on the excellence of your food—as always.'

Her embarrassment increased when her hand was seized and shaken heartily, and trembled when Madame was summoned from the kitchen to receive her due praise also. The handshaking was repeated with enthusiasm, and Marty managed to say shyly, '*La sauce, madame. C'était formidable.*'

Madame replied with voluble pleasure and was clearly waiting for a response. Luc intervened. 'She is asking whether you are a cook?'

'Oh, no.' Marty shook her head. 'I haven't really had any opportunity.'

Madame spoke again, her plump face beaming, and Marty turned rather helplessly to Luc. 'I'm sorry. I couldn't quite catch what she's saying.'

'She says that when you find a man of your own, if you come to her then she will teach you,' he drawled. He paused, then added drily, 'You must thank her, Martine. That is no trifling offer she has just made.'

Marty felt herself flushing again, but she said obediently, '*Vous êtes trop gentille, madame.*'

Madame, apparently satisfied, returned to the kitchen, and Marty subsided, expecting that by this time their table would be the cynosure of all eyes. Yet when she glanced around her, no one seemed to be taking any notice at all. She tried and failed with a giggle to imagine the reaction to a similar scene in the Gardenia Café in the High Street at home.

Luc looked at her, his eyebrows raised enquiringly. 'May I share the joke?'

'There isn't one,' she said hastily. 'Or at least, it wouldn't mean anything to you.'

He gave her a cool, thoughtful look. 'Am I so lacking in humour?'

'No,' she protested awkwardly. It would have been easier, she thought, to explain in the first place.

He went on, his voice cooler than ever. 'You find them amusing, do you—Philippe and Clotilde? They are old friends, you understand, and I did not realise that their warmth, their kindliness would make them objects of derision in your eyes.'

Horrified, she gazed at him. 'Oh, but you're so wrong,' she exclaimed. 'I wasn't laughing at them—I wouldn't. Anyway, there's nothing to laugh at. They're lovely people. It's just all so different from what I'm used to, that's all.' She spread her hands. 'I'll never make you understand.'

'You could if you wished,' he said. His eyes held hers for a moment. 'But there are moments, Martine, when I feel you prefer to shut me out.'

'That's silly,' she said after a moment's pause. 'We—we hardly know each other.'

He took a pack of cigarettes from his pocket and lit one meditatively. 'So you still regard us as strangers?'

'Well—hardly that.' Marty bit her lip. There was an edge to his question that she could not quite comprehend. 'I mean—we're going to be employer and employee?'

'And that contents you?' He was still watching her through the faint cloud of blue smoke now surrounding him.

'Naturally,' she said, hearing and loathing the primness in her voice. 'We—we can hardly be friends—under the circumstances.' She hesitated, waiting for some reaction, but there was none. He simply went on looking at her with an air of polite interest, leaning back in his chair, smoking his cigarette, apparently perfectly relaxed, so why Marty should have this overwhelming impression of a coiled wire spring, she had no idea. She moistened her lips with the tip of her tongue and went on, 'Not that I'm not grateful for all you've done for me. You've been very kind . . .' She blundered to a halt, unnerved by his continuing silence.

'You paint a glowing picture of my virtues, *chérie*,' he said at last, his voice reverting to the sarcastic drawl she so much disliked. 'But I must warn you against being too idealistic, or I might do something to disturb this halo you are thrusting upon me.' His lips twisted. 'And you were clearly correct when you said that we did not know each other. If we had established any kind of *rapport*, you would presumably have told me what you really think instead of uttering these polite platitudes of yours.'

It was his tone rather than the actual words that set the match to her temper.

'Is that a fact?' she said furiously. 'Well, *monsieur*, you can rest easy. I certainly don't regard you as any kind of saint—quite the contrary, in fact. And while I have to be grateful to you for getting me out of a mess, I don't have to take your charity!'

She reached for her handbag with trembling fingers and found the envelope which she tossed across the table to him.

'Nor will I be bought,' she added, her voice trembling.

'And nor do I wish to buy.' His voice cut her to the bone. 'But at least we have the truth at last. Why do you insult me by returning this loan in such a manner?'

'Why did you insult me by giving me so much?' she retorted passionately. 'That wasn't a loan, it was a charitable donation. A loan implies that it has to be repaid. Well, I could never repay that amount of money—not if I worked for you for the rest of my life.'

'A slight exaggeration,' he said coolly. 'And if you allowed yourself to imagine that you were being drawn into a lifetime of well-paid slavery, then you flattered yourself, *chérie*. The job lasts for the summer only, and that is a promise.'

Her face was white now under the lash of his words.

He went on mercilessly, 'As for your other insinuation, *ma mie*, I have never needed to buy a woman yet, so what do you suppose makes you so special?'

'I'm sorry,' she whispered.

'Another platitude.' He smiled mirthlessly. 'My desire for coffee seems to have left me. I think we'll start back.'

He rose to his feet, stubbing out his cigarette in the glass ashtray on the table, then came round to her side. The little striped carrier bag was lying on the chair beside her. He looked at it disdainfully.

'Perhaps I should thank you for condescending to spend at least a little of my money,' he said bitingly, and reached for it, just as her own hand stretched out. The carrier fell to the floor between the chairs, disgorging its contents as it did so.

Luc swore under his breath and dropped to one knee to retrieve it. Marty sat very still, fighting for self-control, aware that now their table was the subject of much interested attention from the other customers.

Luc straightened slowly, his dark brows drawn ominously together. The green bathing suit dangled limply from his hand.

'*Qu'est-ce que c'est que ça?*' he demanded icily.

'You told me I should buy one,' she mumbled defensively.

'But not this.' His frown was positively thunderous as he examined the offending garment more closely. 'Never anything like this!'

'What's wrong with it?' Embarrassed by the scrutiny from the neighbouring tables, Marty picked up her handbag and stood up.

'What is right with it?' he asked bitingly. '*C'est incroyable!*'

'It's a perfectly ordinary bathing costume,' she protested.

'I cannot deny that,' he drawled. 'And for a girl going away to school— or a nun entering a convent—it would no doubt be ideal, but not for you, *ma mie*.' He stuffed the folds of dark green back into the carrier, and pausing only to drop a handful of notes besides the bill on the table, led the way to the door.

In the street, Marty hung back. 'Now where are we going?'

'To exchange this—*naturellement*.' He held up the

carrier, and to her chagrin Marty saw that the name and address of the boutique was emblazoned across it.

'But I don't want to change it,' she persisted, almost having to run to keep up with him. 'It's my choice—you have no right!'

But her words fell on apparently deaf ears. She was still protesting vainly when they arrived back at the boutique which Madame was just reopening after the lunchtime break. Her eyes sharpened with interest when they fell on Luc, and filled with amusement when she saw Marty, flushed with resentment, following him. Within moments it was evident that Luc and Madame were in complete accord, Madame explaining with considerable verve her efforts to dissuade Mademoiselle from the choice she had made. And almost without knowing quite what had happened, Marty found herself back in the little curtained cubicle looking with startled eyes at the reflection of a stranger with dishevelled hair and a bright spot of colour in her cheeks, and whose slender body was enticingly displayed in a series of Madame's briefest bikinis. The merest wisps, some of them, she thought dazedly, lifting the young roundness of her breasts and clinging by a hairsbreadth to the slender curve of her hips. They were sheer provocation, and she knew it. In many ways she would have felt more decent with nothing on at all rather than the semblance of covering that they provided.

And when the curtain was suddenly swept back and Luc was there, his eyes mercilessly assessing her from head to foot, it was as much as she could do not to lift her hands to cover herself from his all-encompassing gaze.

Behind him appeared Madame like a beneficent fairy, her face wreathed in smiles. *'C'est épatant, n'est-ce pas, monsieur?'*

'Formidable,' Luc said slowly. His eyes met Marty's in the mirror, and they held an expression she had never seen in any man's eyes before. A treacherous feeling of weakness assailed her, and she felt as if her legs were dissolving into

water beneath her. For the first time in her life she knew what it was to feel both desirable and desired, and her pulses raced, matching the sudden raggedness of her breathing. She was conscious of a heady mixture of exaltation and fear, aware too that Luc still stood behind her motionless, his eyes holding the mirrored image of hers as if caught in some strange spell of his own devising—and aware also of Madame, her face a discreet mask, but her eyes alive with knowledge and a sly amusement . . .

Marty caught at her reeling senses. She moved suddenly, restlessly, and the spell was broken as she turned.

Luc said quite coolly, 'I think the plain colours, don't you, Martine? The pink, and the emerald, and of course, the black.'

And Madame was eagerly demonstrating that with the black there was also a wrap-around skirt in a swirling pattern of black, white and crimson, and that with the others there were tunics with drawstring necks and loose sleeves, sheer and silky, and Luc was nodding. Marty was conscious of a curious feeling of unreality. She reached abruptly for the cubicle curtain and wrenched it into place, shutting out the boutique and the growing pile of purchases on the counter. All this, she thought desperately, had nothing to do with her. What was she doing here anyway, shut into this small enclosed space with a half-naked stranger whose enormous eyes seemed to be filling the pallor of her face? It was a relief to reach for her own clothes, to have to cope with hooks and zips, and all the small practicalities of getting dressed. It was an effort too to draw back the curtain and re-enter the boutique. The despised green swimsuit was lying discarded at one side. The new purchases already filled two carriers, and the bikini she had just taken off was added to them.

'Merci, monsieur. Merci bien.' Madame showed them to the door, her face beaming with gratification.

Marty walked in silence beside Luc all the way back to the car. She was silent still as he got in beside her and

started the ignition, and as they wound their way out of the
car park and through the traffic to the road that led back to
Les Sables des Pins.

'You're very quiet.' At last he slanted a glance at her.

Marty bit her lip. 'What do you expect?' she asked
tautly, and heard him swear softly and impatiently.

'You strange hostile child,' he said. 'What am I going
to do with you?'

'I see,' she flared. 'So it's all my fault! You—you
humiliate me—and I'm supposed to accept it all with a
sweet smile. Well, thanks, but no thanks!'

His mouth tightened grimly, and without a further word
he applied his brakes and drew the car swiftly and expertly
to a halt at the side of the road in the shade of some trees.

'How am I supposed to have humiliated you?' he stared
in front of him, his hands still gripping the steering wheel.

'Taking me back to that boutique like that,' she said
jerkily. 'Buying me all these things.'

He raised his eyebrows haughtily. 'And what was I supposed to do—simply permit you to disobey my instructions,
in spirit if not in letter? While you are in my employ,
Martine, you will learn to do as I say.'

'There was nothing wrong with my choice,' she defended herself stubbornly.

'There was everything wrong with it.' He pushed an
irritable hand through his hair. 'Why are you so ashamed
of your body? You are neither ugly nor deformed.'

A memory came flooding back of his eyes watching her
in the cubicle mirror, and swift hot colour stained her
cheeks.

'I don't want to discuss it,' she said. 'And I wish you
wouldn't talk to me like that. I don't know what that
woman—the owner of the boutique—must have thought.
She's probably got me written off as one of your Parisian
floozies . . .'

She stopped with a little guilty gasp, her eyes flying to
his face. Whatever had possessed her, she wondered almost

hysterically, to say such a thing? She sounded not only rude, but priggish. It was an Aunt Mary remark from first to last, and her lips were already parting in tentative apology when the storm of anger she saw in his eyes reduced her to a quivering apprehensive silence.

'And is that what you think too, *mignonne*?' His glance locked with hers in a merciless challenge. 'If so, perhaps I should teach you to thank me properly.'

She wanted to jump from the car and run away, anywhere as long as it was out of the reach of his anger—and out of the reach of his arms which were dragging her without gentleness from her seat and across the lean hard warmth of his body. Her hands were imprisoned behind her back, and she was helpless to resist. She looked up into the dark face and blazing eyes now so close to her own and managed to whisper, 'No—please,' before her trembling mouth was claimed by his with utter ruthlessness.

His kiss was devastation, complete and total. He made no allowances for her youth or inexperience, as he plundered the soft sweetness of her mouth, nor did he make any attempt to disguise that his initial anger was now mixed with a rising sensuality.

His long fingers closed on her throat as if to assess for himself her galloping pulse rate, then moved inexorably down. Inside the restrictive cotton of her dress, her small breasts seemed to lift and unfold like sweet summer buds under the insolent sensuous demand of his touch.

His arms were no longer a prison suddenly. He wasn't even kissing her any more. There was nothing to prevent her from pulling away from him, from leaving the car even and obeying her first impulse to run—nothing but this long, slow intimate caress which seemed to be draining her will, her power to resist. She drew a shaky breath. Her mouth was dry, and deep inside her she could feel a slow, shuddering excitement like nothing she had ever experienced before.

Luc's dark gaze seemed to be boring mesmerically into

hers, his brows lifted almost questioningly as he studied her widening eyes, and the parted moistness of her mouth.

Obeying some inner compulsion she barely understood, Marty lifted her arms and slid them round Luc's neck, drawing him down to her again. This time his mouth was gentle on hers, as if he wanted to wipe away the memory of his earlier brutality, but that was his only concession. His kiss demanded an adult response to his lovemaking— a response, the implications of which terrified her and exhilarated her at one and the same time. Even while her senses prompted her almost deliriously, a small voice in the corner of her mind cried out in protest. This was her first kiss—her first embrace. And whatever she had expected or dreamed of from such an event, it had not been this head-long gallop to the heights or the depths of sexual fever. Marty's dreams had been far more tentative affairs, yet at the same time it was as if she had always known this was how Luc's arms would be. That his mouth exploring hers with ever-increasing urgency, his hands caressing her ever more intimately would be able to evoke from her this shuddering, trembling delight that seemed to drive all reason from her.

In her younger days she had read voraciously, often love stories from her aunt's generation and even earlier which were kept in the dining room in a tall glass cupboard. Stories that sometimes dealt with chaste and upright heroines who were seduced by passion from the path of virtue and morality, which Marty who came from a very different generation found frankly ludicrous. Yet at the same time they had always left a question lurking in the back of her mind. Could anyone really be so carried away by their feelings that they became deaf and blind to all promptings except those of their own bodies?

She knew the answer to that now, and the realisation of how passion could bewitch and betray was shaking her to the innermost core of her being. She was even oblivious to the fact that the car was parked only feet from a busy road. All she was aware of was the wild instinctive clamour of her senses, leading her down undreamed of paths.

'*Dieu!*' In the end it was Luc who pulled away, flinging himself back into his seat and pushing his dishevelled dark hair back from his face with a patently unsteady hand. His hands dropped to the steering wheel gripping it as if it was the only reality in a reeling world, and he sat motionless, biting his lower lip until his breathing had steadied.

Marty watched him, her eyes wide and puzzled, feeling suddenly and strangely bereft. She wanted to say something, but coherent words wouldn't form. Instead she put up her hand like a child and touched her swollen mouth. He turned, as if her movement had attracted his attention, and studied her, his look cool and unsmiling.

But his voice was husky. 'You go to my head, *mignonne*,' he said, and reached for the ignition.

'Where are we going?' She was bewildered by the change in him, and ashamed that she could not emulate his coolness. Was he so unmoved by what had just transpired?

He smiled suddenly, a little wryly, then swiftly touched his fingers to his lips and laid them across her own.

'I'm taking you home,' he said quietly. 'Back to Solitaire.' And he drove off into the stream of traffic.

She sat beside him without speaking, still a little dazed by what had happened, her heart thudding painfully. And when they reached Solitaire—what then? she asked herself. What had she invited by her wanton response to his love-making? Hadn't she made it only too clear that he was calling the tune? And now—tonight—if he came to her room, what protest could she make, who had not uttered a word to resist him up to then? And did she even want to protest?

Faint colour rose in her face as the exact tenor of her thoughts came home to her. What in the world was happening to her, she wondered, when she could so calmly contemplate the most intimate of all relationships with a man who was almost a stranger to her? The behaviour she was contemplating was contrary to everything her life had stood for up to that point.

But until now, she thought, I was only half alive.

The journey back to Les Sables seemed endless. She stared at the changing panorama of flat fields and pale yellow sands and small grey towns without really seeing any of it. Her entire consciousness was fixed on the man beside her whose own concentration seemed exclusively concerned with manoeuvring his powerful car along the narrow roads. She wanted very badly to touch him, to put out her hand and rest it lightly on his forearm or his strongly muscled thigh, but she gripped her hands tightly together in her lap to resist the temptation. The time for touching would come later, when he would resume the lesson in loving, begun in anger and ended in desire, and carry it to its natural—its inevitable conclusion. A faint smile touched the corner of her mouth—a happy, dreaming smile—as she acknowledged silently, deep within herself, that she would not have it any other way.

The palms of her hands were sweating slightly as they drove along the road which led to Solitaire and she wiped them unobtrusively on the skirt of her dress. The gate stood open, and she heard Luc make a small impatient noise in his throat as he turned the car in on to the track.

As they rounded the slight bend just before the house, she saw the car standing outside. It was the Citroën that had been there the previous night. She leaned forward, staring through the windscreen, and saw its owner emerge from the house and stand beside it, lifting an arm as she smiled a greeting. Luc parked his own car behind hers and got out. He walked round to the passenger side and helped Marty to alight. His hand under her arm was wholly impersonal, and as she looked up at him, she saw he was looking over her head at the woman.

'*Bonjour*, Gisèle,' he said. 'What a pleasant surprise!'

The woman called Gisèle lifted a lazy shoulder. She looked cool and elegant in a shirtwaister in some silky olive green material and her hair and make-up were immaculate.

Marty stood in the shadow of Luc's car clutching her carrier bags and feeling hot and dishevelled. She saw Gisèle's eyes travel slowly and dismissively over her, and a faint smile curved the exquisitely painted lips.

She said reproachfully, 'But why did you not tell me you were going to La Rochelle, *chéri*? I would have come with you. So this is your little *protégée*. How old did you say she was?'

It was very skilfully done, Marty realised as she made herself control her temper. Even though her French was not fluent, she was left in no doubt as to exactly what the newcomer meant, and where she was considered to fit into the scheme of things.

Luc said pleasantly in English, 'I don't think I discussed her age at all. Gisèle, may I present Mademoiselle Martine Langton. Martine, this is Madame Andry.'

The older woman extended her hand and Marty allowed her fingers to be held for a moment in her cool, unwelcoming clasp. Gisèle Andry's cordial smile did not reach as far as her eyes, but to the casual observer she was all charm.

'Welcome to Les Sables, *mademoiselle*. I hope you will be happy while you stay with us,' she enunciated carefully in heavily accented English, and Marty wondered whether her use of pronoun was deliberate. She was aware of Madame Andry's eyes resting thoughtfully on her flushed face, and she wondered miserably whether the glow which had transfused her all the way home was still visible, and if Gisèle Andry was quite well aware that Luc had been making love to her.

Madame Andry stepped past her and went to Luc, sliding her arm through his with deliberate intimacy and smiling up into his face.

'I need a drink, *mon ami*,' she said with pretty plaintiveness. 'I have an insupportable thirst.'

'But of course.' He turned to Marty. 'Would you like to join us?'

Marty found herself avoiding his gaze. She said in a low voice. 'No, thank you, monsieur. I'll just take these things up to my room. I—I'm rather tired, and I think I'll rest before dinner.'

He shrugged. 'As you wish.'

She went past them and into the house. As she crossed the hall, she found she was nursing the vague hope that Luc would come after her on some pretext or other, and that he would say something to her—something reassuring at least. But she mounted the stairs and walked along the gallery to her room quite alone. She tossed her packages on to the bed and walked listlessly across the room to adjust the shutters. They were still standing there below her.

Gisèle Andry's voice was quite audible as it floated upwards in the still, warm air. It was husky with amusement.

'So no one is safe from you, *chéri*. Not even a little English mouse. How you are abominable!'

She stepped forward into his arms and raised her laughing mouth for his kiss.

CHAPTER SIX

MARTY lay across the bed, staring sightlessly up at the immaculate whiteness of the ceiling. The first bitter ache of humiliation had subsided, but her skin felt oddly sore, almost as if Madame Andry had raked her elegantly shaped nails across the surface. The old childhood jingle 'Sticks and stones may break my bones, but words can never hurt me' echoed and re-echoed tauntingly inside her head. Not so, she thought bewilderedly. Not so. A broken limb would pain, but the pain would be clean and sharp. Words that were deliberately uttered to hurt—and she had little doubt that Gisèle Andry who had seen her at the window the night before had intended her to hear her laughing remark—lingered like scum across the pool of memory.

She moved swiftly, almost defensively, feeling the shaming colour burning its way back into her face.

She had no idea what the time was, but to judge by the lengthening shadows across the floor, evening must be approaching. She shivered slightly, drawing her wrap more closely round her body.

Her first action, after stepping back stricken from the window, had been to walk, her body held stiffly like an automaton, across to the tiny bathroom. She had stripped, hurling her few clothes uncaringly to the floor, and then stepped under the shower, allowing the water to stream over her entire body, drenching her and stinging her eyes.

Water cleansed, she told herself. Water healed. She wanted to wash all the memory of this day away from her—all of it—Luc's eyes watching her in the mirror, his mouth exploding into angry passion on hers, and his hands—ah, dear God, that most of all—his too-knowing, too-expert hands on her body. Maybe when she had completed this

ritual with water, she would feel clean and whole again.
Maybe.

Nothing was certain any more, least of all her own feelings. And she had no excuse. She had sensed from the first
that almost frightening attraction that Luc Dumarais possessed for her. She had sensed it and done less than nothing
to fight against it. She had walked into today's situation
with her eyes wide open, ignoring the powerful warnings
of her instinct. She had allowed it to develop—might even
involuntarily have prompted it. Luc Dumarais had warned
her, after all, of the dangers of provocation where he was
concerned.

She had dried herself carelessly, applying the rough
surface of the towel fiercely to her slender body. She did
not bother about her soaking hair, merely winding a dry
towel round it turban-wise, before returning to the bedroom and throwing herself across the bed. Then she had
begun to shiver.

Yes, she had been warned, but words had not been
enough. Like a reckless child wanting proof that a fire
burns, she had stretched out her hands to the blaze, and
who could she blame but herself if she had been scorched
in the process?

She rolled restlessly on to her stomach, and rested her
chin moodily on her folded hands. She was being foolishly
melodramatic, she told herself. After all, nothing had happened but a little casual lovemaking. Judging by what
Madame Andry had said, such incidents were common in
Luc Dumarais' progress through life. Obviously the older
woman did not find the idea as repellent as Marty did.
Perhaps, she thought, her lips twisting disgustedly, it even
added a fillip to their own relationship, and she could be in
no doubt about what that was. It was written large in every
word, every smile, every gesture, every mark of possession.
And she had allowed herself to think for one small moment
that Luc found her more than merely fleetingly desirable.
In fact, all she had been, she told herself flatly, was a brief

diversion in the absence of his mistress. Perhaps that was
how Gisèle Andry regarded it too, and that was why she
was able to view his behaviour with such composure. She
must have every confidence in her ability to always come
first with Luc, no matter how often his eyes might stray,
she thought achingly. In any case, a woman of Gisèle's
beauty and sophistication could have no fear of being sup-
planted by an immature girl.

And presently she would have to go downstairs and face
them both at dinner, and pretend with all her might that
those brief, burning moments in Luc's arms hadn't mat-
tered to her either.

Either that, or she would have to leave. But how could
she do so, when she was now in Luc's debt quite practically? Besides, flight would be a tacit admission of the
devastation Luc had caused to her peace of mind, and the
thought of them laughing at her, perhaps even pitying her
after her departure was frankly unbearable. She owed it to
herself, she thought, to face them, so that she could take
her leave after her summer at Solitaire was over with at
least some rags of self-respect.

Someone rapped sharply at the door, and she tensed.
Perhaps the choice was not to be hers, she thought as she
slipped off the bed, tying the belt of her wrap more
securely. Perhaps this was Luc come to tell her that to save
further embarrassment he was dispensing with her services
and sending her back to England.

And with an aching pang of self-revelation she knew
suddenly just how much any such decision on his part
would now cost her.

It took all the courage of which she was capable to open
the door with a calm face, but it was not Luc who stood
there but Madame Guisard, enquiring tartly when she was
coming downstairs for her meal.

'I'm sorry,' Marty apologised awkwardly, her face flushing as Madame's sharp eyes gave her obvious state of undress a critical glance. 'I didn't know—am I keeping Mon-

sieur—and Madame waiting?'

The housekeeper lifted a shoulder in a shrug. 'It is my-self who awaits you, *mademoiselle*,' she retorted coldly. 'Monsieur is dining with friends this evening.'

She turned away, and Marty stood staring after her, not knowing whether to be glad or sorry about the information which she had so surlily imparted. It was true she had not relished the idea of sharing a dinner table with Luc and his mistress, but Aunt Mary had always insisted there was nothing to be gained by deferring awkward or difficult situations, and Marty had always tended to agree with her. Yet once again the choice had not been hers to make.

Dining with friends, she thought, and no doubt Gisèle would make one of the party. Perhaps it might even be at her house, although Madame Guisard's discretion as Luc's housekeeper would not reveal as much. Whatever form the evening might take, it was certain that their relationship was an accepted one. They had mutual friends, perhaps they were even expected to marry one day. Maybe they had only deferred the actual ceremony waiting for a time when Bernard's behaviour might have become more amenable. Gisèle Andry had not the appearance of a woman who would take kindly to a surly stepson. Candidly, Marty found herself thinking as she turned back into the room and closed the door, Gisèle Andry did not seem the step-mother type—if there was such a thing—in any way, although she was prepared to admit that her own emotional involvement was probably affecting the fairness of her judgment.

The Mexican print was still lying in a crumpled heap on the floor where she had discarded it, and she pushed it aside with one foot, her lips tightening. How long would it be, she wondered as she resumed the jeans and top she had worn earlier that day, before the sight of the dress would cease to set her memory functioning wildly? She ran a perfunctory comb through her still damp tendrils of hair and grimaced at herself in the mirror. Wet hair, no make-

up, and a distinct lack of feminine curves. Every inch the
English mouse that Gisèle Andry had dismissed her as, and
perhaps it would be a safe façade for her to shelter behind
while she remained in France.

She was making for the patio when she got downstairs,
but Madame Guisard's harsh voice soon recalled her. It
seemed there were to be no alfresco meals for the hired
help in the absence of Monsieur, Marty thought resignedly
as she followed the housekeeper's figure across the hall into
a smaller room attractively panelled in pine, and dominated
by an elegant circular dining table at which a place had
been set for one.

Marty halted staring at the solitary place setting. '*Bernard n'est pas ici?*' she asked haltingly. '*Il accompagne son
père, peut-être?*'

Madame's grim, almost contemptuous smile dismissed
any such notion. Bernard, she announced curtly, was once
again dining in his room.

'Then I think I'll join him,' Marty said, repelled by the
implications of her solitary state in the dining room. 'Perhaps you could put my food on a tray, *madame*.'

The request was courteously made, but at the same time
Marty lifted her chin, and any arguments that Madame
Guisard might have been mustering against the incon-
venience of such a course of action were confined to a dis-
gruntled mutter of acquiescence.

Left to herself while the housekeeper went off to fetch
the tray, Marty supposed that Bernard was being punished
yet again by being sent to his room. She realised that she
ought not to interfere with some probably necessary disci-
pline, but on the other hand she had to try and get to
know Bernard if she was to go any way towards earning
the salary Luc Dumarais was paying her.

Accordingly when Madame Guisard returned with the
tray, she thanked her demurely, ignoring her expression of
tight-lipped disapproval which seemed endemic as far as
she was concerned, she thought wryly as she mounted the

stairs, holding the tray steadily.

She remembered that Bernard had said he occupied the room next to hers, and balancing the tray on her arm, she knocked at the door.

For a moment there was silence and she thought that he might be asleep, then a voice called grudgingly, '*Entrez*!'

Marty took a deep breath, then opened the door with an air of breezy confidence that she was far from feeling.

'*Bonsoir*, Bernard,' she greeted the rather forlorn figure curled up on the window seat. 'It was a bit lonely downstairs, so I thought I'd come up and eat with you—if you don't mind.'

The boy moved his shoulders with an air of resignation. '*Si vous voulez, mademoiselle.*' His voice conveyed utter indifference as to whether she stayed or went, but Marty held determinedly on to her smile. She set the tray down on a small table against the wall which seemed to double as a writing desk, and drew up a chair.

'Have you eaten already?' she asked.

'I was not hungry.'

Probably still recovering from his raid on the larder this morning, Marty thought rather tartly, but she could not help relenting when she saw the shadows under his eyes and the pinched look round his mouth. Bernard was genuinely unhappy, there was no doubt. Well, that was something she could understand. She was unhappy herself. That surely gave them some common ground on which to build even a temporary relationship.

'Where did you go today?' she asked as she began on the egg mayonnaise.

'To the beach.'

'Is that where you always go?'

'Why do you wish to know?' Bernard demanded irritably. 'Has Papa required that you follow me?'

Marty laid down her fork and stared at him. Then she said quietly and evenly, 'No, he has not. And I don't really wish to know where you go or in fact anything about you.

I was merely being polite—trying to make conversation. It's clearly something you're not used to. We're both on our own. I would have been glad of some company, and thought you might feel the same. Obviously I was mistaken. Goodnight, Bernard.'

She picked up the tray. She was almost at the door when a subdued voice from behind her said:

'I—I'm sorry, *mademoiselle*. *Je vous demande pardon*. Please stay.'

Marty turned slowly. The anxiety on his face made him look suddenly very small and young.

She said gently, 'I'm not here to spy on you, Bernard—you must believe that. But I'd be a liar if I pretended that your—your father wouldn't like us to be friends. I hoped it might be possible too. That's the reason I agreed to stay.'

She returned to the table and sat down.

'So you are going to let Papa use you—like he uses everyone,' he said after a minute or two.

She supposed she ought to reprove him for such a speech, but after all she wasn't employed as his governess, and she wouldn't gain his confidence by carping at him. If he genuinely felt these things, perhaps it would be good therapy for him to speak them aloud rather than let them fester secretly in his mind.

She gave a little shrug, and applied herself once more to the egg mayonnaise. 'Hardly,' she said. 'He's providing me with a very generous salary.'

'Just to talk to me?' He sounded sceptical.

'No. I have some secretarial work to do as well.' She gave him a level look. 'I won't pretend to you, Bernard. I'm grateful to your father. He's helping me out of a pretty nasty mess.'

The implication, unspoken, hovered between them that Bernard knew exactly who was responsible for at least part of that mess, and he had the grace to blush.

'But he'll use you just the same,' he muttered. 'He will use your gratitude and your attraction for him.'

Whatever she had been expecting him to say, it certainly hadn't been that. She stared at him helplessly, feeling the betraying blush rising in her face.

'I don't know what you mean,' she said weakly at last, abandoning all pretence of coping with the egg mayonnaise.

Bernard's smile was both adult and superior. 'I saw the way you looked at him yesterday—as if the sun had dazzled you,' he explained kindly. 'Women have always looked at him so.'

'You are hardly in a position to know that,' Marty pointed out austerely, still hot with embarrassment.

He shrugged. 'It was what my mother told me,' he said briefly, and Marty's gaze widened in consternation at the bitterness the few words barely concealed.

Bernard observed her curiously. '*Qu'avez-vous?* It shocks you that my mother should speak of such things to me?'

Marty swallowed. 'Yes—I suppose.'

'She wished me to know the truth,' he said simply. 'Papa and women—it was always so.'

There was a silence. Marty sat staring down at the table. She was deeply conscious that this was not the end of the conversation, that Bernard wanted it to continue, and that she owed it to him to go along with this however personally painful she might find the subject.

At last she said, 'Is—is that why she left him?'

'She did not leave him,' Bernard said. 'He left her.'

'For another woman?' Marty did not look at Bernard as she probed. Each question afflicted her like the twist of a knife.

'For no particular woman,' said the young/old child's voice. 'You see, he wearied of her, *mademoiselle*. She no longer had appeal for him.'

Marty moved swiftly, restlessly. 'Perhaps you shouldn't tell me any more,' she began.

'If you are to stay in this house then there are things you must know,' Bernard said unanswerably. He gave her a narrow-eyed, unsmiling look. 'Though you have probably nothing to fear. You are not beautiful enough for Papa to be interested in you. Besides, he has a mistress already.'

'So I gather,' Marty said half under her breath, and wished the words unsaid, afraid that Bernard would recognise with unchildlike perception the emotions she was trying to conceal.

But perhaps he had not heard her, because he went on, 'My mother was very beautiful when she was young. Would you like to see a photograph of her?'

'Do you have one?' Marty glanced round the room. It seemed bare of the usual clutter, and she could see no pictures of any kind.

'It is here.' He came over to the table where she was sitting and opened a drawer beneath its flap, extracting a large leather-covered album. Bernard opened it and Marty saw that it was not a photograph album in the conventional sense, but rather a book of press cuttings. All of them, she saw, dealing with the career of a young actress called Victorine Cajoux.

'*Voici ma mère*,' said Bernard, and for a moment the tremble in his voice made him totally a child again.

Almost in spite of herself, Marty began to examine the yellowing cuttings. There were some photographs as well, she saw, obviously publicity shots taken with the soft focus, which only served to emphasise the warm sensual beauty of the girl who looked up at them both. Yes, she was lovely, Marty acknowledged, but what had set Victorine Cajoux apart from other glamorous French starlets must have been that vibrant sexuality of hers which shone undimmed even from an elderly still photograph. Encountering that combination of innocence and experience in the flesh must have been dynamite, Marty thought, rather like seeing the eyes of a *fille de joie* in the face of a novice nun. The analogy made her feel suddenly uncomfortable and she turned the page aware that her hand was shaking a little.

'*Elle était belle, n'est-ce pas?*' She stared a little at the

sound of Bernard's voice close to her ear. She had forgotten
that he was still standing next to her, but she could not
overlook the note of pleading in his voice.

'Very beautiful,' she said gently. 'I don't blame you for
being proud of her, Bernard. I'm afraid I don't know very
much about films. Was she very successful?'

'Yes.' Bernard sat down on the carpet and leaned back
against the leg of the table. 'She had a little success alone,
and then my father found her and married her. He was becoming known as a young director then and they made
some films together that were a *succès fou*. Some said like
Vadim and Bardot, *vous savez*.' His voice roughened. 'Then
Maman discovered that was all he wanted of her. That she
continued to be beautiful for these films that he would
make with her, but nothing else. When she told him that
she wanted a home—children, he laughed at her. And when
she told him that she was *enceinte*'—he peered up at Marty
—'*Vous comprenez ça?*'

'Yes,' Marty said numbly. 'She told him she was preg-
nant.'

'*Oui*. He was—very angry. Because he did not want a
child, he said that she should not want one either. He said
that she would lose her beauty, her mystery—that mother-
hood would make her commonplace.' He paused, and it
came home to Marty for the first time that it was his own
small, unwanted presence he was referring to. She sank her
teeth into her lower lip and waited for him to go on.

'They quarrelled,' said the quiet voice. 'Each night, they
quarrelled. He would tell her that she was becoming gross
—hideous, that her body would be ruined for ever. He
wanted her to get rid of the baby.'

'Oh, no, Bernard!' Marty was beginning to feel physically sick. 'Please don't tell me any more.'

'There is not much to tell,' he said flatly. 'I was born,
and to an extent, my father was right. Maman's figure was
never the same as it had been before, and the roles she had
played before were offered to her no longer. My father told

her that she had become repulsive. He would go away—stay away for weeks and not tell her where he had been. But she knew—because of the stories in the newspapers. And she would know whom he had been with and suffer. At last he did not come back.'

There was no emotion in his voice as he completed the sordid little recital and sat silent, staring down at his slippered feet.

Marty wanted to say something—something wise and profound and mature beyond her years, but not a single word occurred to her. She sat, staring down at a knot-hole in the wooden surface of the table and willing herself not to cry.

'So do you now wonder, *mademoiselle*,' said the boy at her feet, 'why I do not wish to reside with my papa?'

She shook her head, feeling that a verbal reply was beyond her.

Bernard scrambled to his feet and stood playing with the cord of his dressing gown for a moment.

'You are not going to eat your food?' he asked almost solicitously, his dark eyes going over the loaded tray.

Again she shook her head, this time managing a rueful smile as well.

'I'm not very hungry either,' she said quietly.

He went on fidgeting with his dressing gown cord.

'Tomorrow, if you wish, I will show you the beach,' he said at last.

'I'd like that very much,' said Marty. She rose to her feet, grimacing at the tray with an effort at lightheartedness. 'I suppose I'd better dispose of the evidence before Madame Guisard scolds me.'

He shrugged. 'Give it to César. He has an appetite of the most stupendous. And Albertine will not scold you. You are the relation of her beloved Monsieur Langton, *vous savez bien*.'

Marty paused, her attention arrested. 'But I thought she was your father's housekeeper.'

'She is now, of course, but before that she worked for Jacques. When he died, *mon père* suggested that she should remain here and work for him.' He paused, then said reluctantly, 'I think he was sorry for her because she had been left so little, and there was a time, I think, when she expected that your uncle would marry her.'

'Marry her?' Marty was startled. Quite apart from anything else, it was strange to think of the grim-faced Madame Guisard arousing the tender passion in anyone's bosom, including the late Monsieur Guisard. Besides, Uncle Jim had been in love with her mother; she was convinced that he had. Could loneliness really have forced him to turn to such a very different type of woman and consider matrimony at last?

'You did not know this?' Bernard persisted.

'No, I didn't,' Marty confessed. But it could explain a lot, she thought silently. Perhaps the only thing afflicting Madame Guisard was common or garden jealousy. She might have deluded herself that she was the only person in the world that Uncle Jim cared for, or who cared for him. If that was the case, then her own arrival on the scene must have been an unpleasant blow for the woman. Marty decided that she would never like Madame Guisard, or be able to understand what Uncle Jim had seen in her, apart, of course, from her cooking, but in future she would regard her with a slightly more sympathetic eye for Uncle Jim's sake.

Marty did not sleep well that night, but she had not expected to. She lay tossing restlessly, her mind going round and round in circles on a despairing treadmill. She could not doubt Bernard's sincerity. The story he had related had been told almost dispassionately, as if he was trying in some obscure way to dissociate himself from it, and she could not blame him for this. In a way, it seemed that he had been used as an excuse by both his parents—by his father to end a relationship which had become stale, and by his mother, to explain the sudden failure of her career. It was an unenviable situation for any child, and Bernard's strange behaviour became more understandable.

Marty sighed. Did Luc Dumarais actually expect her to achieve some miracle of reconciliation after all that had happened? Even if Bernard's story was an exaggeration—if his mother had added some bitter embroidery of her own to the facts, there must nevertheless be a grain of truth in it.

She could hear Bernard's voice saying, 'He will use you,' and later, 'You are not beautiful enough for Papa to be interested in.'

Perhaps that was the answer to that brief unsatisfactory interlude in the car. She annoyed Luc, she provoked him, so she had to be shown who was the master, drawn into the dark web of his attraction. Perhaps his conquests had taught him that even a few minutes of casual lovemaking were enough to make most women his slaves—and that a little English mouse, untouched and unawakened, would be a pushover.

She turned over and buried her face in the pillow, trying to seek oblivion in the burning darkness. Poor little Bernard, caught between a womanising father who had never really wanted him, and an embittered beauty who all too probably blamed him for the loss of her looks.

In spite of the confusion her own emotions had been thrown into by his story, she was nevertheless glad that she had decided to stay. At least she could provide him with some sort of companionship for a while, although she realised she would have to beware of building up too strong a relationship if the opportunity arose. She must realise that her time at Solitaire was strictly limited. When the autumn came, her services would be dispensed with, and she did not want to cause Bernard more unhappiness than he had already suffered.

She gave a little muffled groan. It was an impossible position to be in, and she did not feel she had either the experience or the maturity to cope with it. All she could do

was take one step at a time and hope and pray that she
would not do too much harm.

She looked pale and heavy-eyed the following morning,
and she pinched at her cheeks desperately in front of the
mirror, trying to induce some colour into them before
venturing downstairs. The last thing she wanted was Luc
Dumarais to think she had spent a sleepless night because
of what had passed between them, and she did not feel
capable of telling him the true reason for her restlessness.

It was late when she got downstairs and the dining room
table was littered with cups and crumbs, showing that both
Luc and his son had breakfasted before her. She halted in
the doorway, staring at the empty room and feeling rather
at a loss. Bernard's absence worried her. She hoped he had
not had second thoughts about his offer to show her the
beach. Perhaps he was regretting his frankness of the previous night.

Her unhappy train of thought was interrupted by the
arrival of Madame Guisard with fresh *croissants* and a pot
of coffee which she placed on the table with a bad-tempered
thump.

'I'm sorry I'm late,' said Marty, and could not resist
adding, 'Yesterday I was too early. Perhaps tomorrow I'll
get it just right.'

'Perhaps tomorrow you will not be here,' Madame
Guisard said with a kind of grim triumph. 'Monsieur
wishes to speak with you in the *salon* after you have
finished your breakfast.'

Her tone suggested that the best Marty could hope for
from the forthcoming interview was instant dismissal.

The prospect of having to face Luc, coupled with the
fact that she had eaten almost nothing the previous night,
made Marty linger over the *croissants*. They were delici-
ously flaky and still warm, and the jam which accompanied
them had an appetising tartness. Marty ate her fill and
drained the coffee pot dry before rising reluctantly and
brushing a few remaining crumbs from her jeans.

She walked slowly across the hall and knocked on the *salon* door. Luc's *'Entrez'* sounded abrupt, and Marty swallowed before obeying.

He was standing by the window holding an open newspaper which he appeared to be scanning.

'Bonjour, Martine.' His greeting was bleak. 'So here you are at last.'

'I'm sorry if I've kept you waiting.' He had not asked her to sit down, but she took a seat on the sofa facing the fire and looked up at him. It occurred to her that he too looked as if he had not slept very well, and a sudden flush suffused her face as she realised what the circumstances of his sleeplessness had probably been.

'You don't look well,' he said abruptly.

'I'm fine,' she returned with pseudo-brightness. 'Although it's kind of you to be concerned over my health. Is that all you wanted to ask me about?'

He did not bother to conceal the irritation in his voice. 'You know quite well that it is not,' he said. 'Surely it must have occurred to you that after what happened—yesterday, I would have to talk to you.'

Her pulses were pounding, and she felt a faint beading of sweat at her temples, but she put her head on one side, pretending to stare rather blankly in front of her.

'What happened yesterday?' she questioned vaguely, and then, as if light had suddenly dawned, 'Oh, *that*! Oh, I *see*.'

'Yes, *that*,' he mimicked sarcastically. 'Surely you realised we have something to discuss.'

She made herself meet his eyes. 'I don't really see why,' she said coolly. 'After all, what did happen? You kissed me. It was no big deal.'

There was a small crackling silence, then he said, a level of controlled anger underlying his quiet tone, 'It was a little more than just a kiss, I think.'

Marty rose to her feet in one swift, graceful gesture. She said, 'That's all it was to me, *monsieur*. And you needn't fear that I shall forget my place as your employee because of it.' She paused to steady her voice, then went on, 'Besides, we both know it won't happen again. You've satisfied your masculine ego by making the obligatory pass. I suppose you were afraid that my lack of experience might interpret your advances as a declaration of love.'

She stopped with a little gasp, realising that she had gone too far. Luc was looking at her, and there was an ominous white line round his mouth. At his sides, his hands were clenching and unclenching, and she had the sudden crazy feeling that he wished they were around her neck. She took a step backwards.

She would have no one to blame but herself if he did sack her, she thought. She might well find herself thrown out into the road, bag and baggage.

'You have a viper's tongue, Martine,' he said at last, and the smile which accompanied his words was not a pleasant one. 'But why back away? Are you afraid that I shall perhaps offer you violence? But I shall not. As you said, I have made the obligatory pass, and I really have not the slightest desire to touch you again even to give you the thrashing you so much deserve.'

When he had finished speaking, the only sound Marty could hear in the room was her own ragged breathing.

She said unevenly, 'My God, I hate you!'

Then the door to the *salon* was flung wide and Bernard came in exclaiming impatiently, 'Aren't you ready, *mademoiselle*? I have been waiting for you since forever!'

'Yes, I'm sorry, Bernard.' Marty turned to him thankfully, recognising the sudden snapping of the tension which his arrival had enforced. 'I'm coming now. That is if Monsieur has finished with me?'

She glanced back towards Luc, biting her lip as she encountered his gaze.

'No,' he said quietly and chillingly, 'I have not finished with you, Martine, but it will keep—I promise you that. I wish you both a pleasant day.'

He walked past them both and went out of the *salon* closing the door behind him.

Bernard's eyes were bright with curiosity as they rested on Marty.

'Have you been quarrelling with Papa?'

'Of course not.' She gave an unconvincing laugh. 'What makes you think that?'

He shrugged. 'You both looked so strange when I came in, and Papa spoke very quietly, which he does when he is very angry. Other people shout, but he just speaks quietly.'

Marty hesitated. 'Well, to tell the truth, Bernard, I don't think your papa is very pleased with me just at the moment.'

Bernard stared at her. '*Pourquoi pas?* He is not pleased perhaps because we go to the beach?'

'No, oh, no.' Marty shook her head. 'It has nothing to do with you at all.'

Bernard seemed unconsoled by the assurance. 'That is a pity,' he said flatly. 'I tell myself that if I make Papa sufficiently angry he will send be back to Paris to remain with the family of my mother.' He glanced at Marty sideways. 'Perhaps it would be better if I ran away again.'

'Oh no, you don't, young man,' Marty said grimly, and took his arm. 'For today at least, we're going to stick to each other like glue. Besides,' she added, pretending to frown, 'if you don't show me the way to the beach, I might get lost.'

Bernard grinned cheerfully enough. 'That is foolishness, I think,' he pronounced. 'I will go and get some food from the kitchen while you change.'

'Just a minute.' Marty detained him. 'I think we'll go to the kitchen together and ask Madame Guisard to make us up a picnic basket. She was very angry last night because you took some food without asking.'

Bernard gave Marty another of his sideways glances. This time, however, it was disturbingly sly. 'Perhaps,' he said noncommittally. 'However, we will ask, if that is what you wish.'

'It is indeed,' Marty assured him.

A few minutes later she was back in her room, shedding her jeans and top and putting on the emerald green bikini, and the flimsy hip-length tunic that went with it. She thrust a folded towel and her comb into her shoulder bag, and added a purse containing a few francs. She had never felt less like a day on the beach in her life.

She could see the expression in Luc's eyes and hear the terrifying note in his voice as he promised her that there would be a reckoning between them, and she shivered involuntarily.

If she could have obeyed her instincts at that moment, she would have thrown her few belongings back into her suitcase and taken off. Hitch-hiked to Paris, perhaps, and thrown herself on the mercy of the British Embassy to get her back to England.

But she could not do that, because downstairs a young and very confused boy was waiting for her. A boy who had trusted her with his confidence, for whom another rebuff might well prove intolerable.

She drew a trembling breath. One step—one day at a time, she would stay at Solitaire for Bernard's sake. And perhaps if she repeated that a sufficient number of times, she would in the end come to believe it.

CHAPTER SEVEN

THE green mint-flavoured drink was tinglingly cool and refreshing and Marty sipped at it gratefully. In the two weeks since she had arrived at Les Sables des Pins, there had been no sign of even the slightest break in the hot weather. In fact, if it hadn't been for that faint cool breeze from the sea, Marty thought she would probably have begun to find the constant glare of the sun against the cloudless blue sky rather oppressive.

Her daily swimming and sunbathing sessions with Bernard had led to her skin acquiring a smooth golden tan, and she was no longer self-conscious about the pallor of her appearance among the deeply browned French holidaymakers who now thronged the little town. *Le mois d'août* was in full swing, and everyone, it seemed, was taking full advantage of it—everyone, that was, except Luc Dumarais, who seemed totally unconscious of the holiday season and had thrown himself into his work with tight-lipped unrelenting preoccupation.

As always, the merest thought of Luc was enough to bring a shadow to Marty's face and she set down her glass with a barely suppressed sigh. For several days after their confrontation in the *salon* she had waited with trepidation each time their paths crossed for a resumption of hostilities. But Luc seemed in no hurry to enforce the threat implicit in his parting words to her. Indeed, most of the time he behaved as if she did not exist.

Each day after breakfast, he went into his study at the back of the house and closed the door, the very gesture making it clear that all interruptions would be unwelcome. Marty supposed he emerged at lunchtime to eat in solitary splendour on the patio or in the dining room, but she had no concrete knowledge of this. She and Bernard were usually still on the beach at midday, or—as today—in Les Sables des Pins so that Bernard could spend some of his allowance on paperback books.

Sometimes Luc joined them for dinner in the evenings, but more often Marty would see the sleek lines of the car disappearing down the track as evening came. She had no idea where he went or how he spent his time, and she tried to tell herself that she was glad of this. Certainly for her own peace of mind, it was safer not to know. But ignorance, she had discovered with some desperation, could not stop her wondering or caring.

In spite of the remote rather formal hostility that marked his manner when they were thrown into each other's company, and, more drastically, in spite of everything Bernard had told her about him, she was still deeply aware of him with every fibre of her being. The evenings he spent away from the villa were a torture to her. Often she lay in bed, wakeful into the small hours, waiting for the soft growl of the returning engine and the sudden blare of headlights through the slats of the shutters.

Nothing more had been said about her doing any secretarial work for him, and Marty could only suppose miserably that the idea of her working in close proximity with him had become repugnant to him. To her dismay, she realised that while it might have been hurtful to be the target for one of his fleeting and casual *amours*, it was even more hurtful to be ignored by him.

On the brighter side, her relationship with Bernard seemed to be developing along the right lines. She wondered sometimes if he regretted taking her quite so fully into his confidence on short acquaintance. Certainly he never referred again to his parents' marriage and the circumstances of its breakdown, although she had given him ample opportunities.

But he was prepared to talk about Jim Langton, and the months before his death. He had evidently been very fond of the older man and spent a lot of time in his company, at first, she guessed, so that he could avoid his father, but later for Uncle Jim's own sake.

She learned too that Uncle Jim had stayed on at Solitaire, even after its sale to Luc Dumarais, acting as a kind of caretaker during Luc's trips to Paris and elsewhere. She had also guessed, although he would never openly admit it, that it was Bernard who provided the flowers for Uncle Jim's grave in the pinewoods.

She had tried to press Bernard further on his allegation that Madame Guisard had expected to become Uncle Jim's wife, but he became irritatingly vague on the subject, suggesting that she should tackle Madame herself on the subject.

But this Marty did not feel disposed to do. The passage of time since her arrival at Solitaire had not softened Madame's attitude towards her one jot, and Marty could guess at the sort of reaction she could expect if she dared raise the question with the housekeeper of her exact relationship with her former employer. At the very least, she would get a furious rebuff.

And really, Marty tried to tell herself charitably, it isn't any of my business. It's enough that I know that she and Uncle Jim had the prospect of some happiness. I oughtn't to probe any further. Nevertheless it was another nagging question mark hanging over her life at the villa.

Marty shifted on her slatted wooden seat. Bernard was taking longer over his tour of the bookshops than he had promised, she thought, glancing at her watch. She had finished her drink and was beginning to grow restive, but if she went in search of him, she might well miss him in the crowds that filled the narrow streets, and they would spend the remainder of the hot afternoon hunting each other. It was easier to remain where she was, and hope that he would turn up before common decency forced her to order another drink from the waiter, or the group of young men at the next table decided she was a fair target for their cheerful, extrovert attentions.

Damn! One of them was already coming over. Embarrassed, Marty bent to retrieve her handbag from the pavement beside her chair, and was amazed to hear a voice above her say in English:

'So we meet again! It is you, is it not Martine?'

She glanced up bewildered and recognised Jean-Paul, the young student who had given her a lift to Solitaire on the day of her arrival.

'You permit?' he enquired, and without waiting for a reply drew out the chair next to hers and sat down, summoning the waiter with an experienced flick of his fingers. 'How nice that I see you after so long. You will have a drink with me, *non*?' He eyed the vividly coloured dregs in her glass with an experienced eye. 'You wish for another *Diaboule à menthe*, or would you prefer something a little stronger—*un pineau, peut-être*—or a beer?'

Marty hesitated. A refusal would seem churlish in the face of all this determined goodwill, although she had to decline the rather battered packet of Gauloises he proffered towards her.

'*Diaboule à menthe* would be fine,' she said with another glance at her watch. 'I haven't a great deal of time, actually. I'm supposed to be meeting someone here.'

Jean-Paul grimaced. '*C'est dommage.* And I had hoped you would have some time for me.'

He contrived to make it sound as if a life's ambition had been dashed to the ground, and Marty was forced to smile. His attentions might be insincere, but they were flattering just the same, and she wouldn't have been human if she had not known a small glow of pleasure at the thought that an attractive young man had sought her out to flirt with.

'And the visit to Solitaire.' Jean-Paul leaned back in his chair and blew out a cloud of pungent blue smoke. 'The *rendezvous* with the good uncle. How did that go?'

She saw there was an amused look in his half-closed eyes.

'You know perfectly well that Luc Dumarais is not my uncle,' she said stiffly.

'One had suspicions, *c'est vrai*, but in this world what is not possible?' Jean-Paul asked largely. 'And the real uncle. Where is he?'

Marty stared down at the drinks the waiter was putting in front of them. 'He died—quite some time ago,' she returned in a constricted voice.

'Ah, *pardon*.' Jean-Paul was silent for a moment.

Marty looked at him. 'You didn't know?'

Jean-Paul spread out his hands. 'How could I have done so?'

'Well,' she said slowly, 'you mentioned something about Madame Guisard being the aunt of someone you knew. She worked for my uncle before she was employed by Monsieur Dumarais. In fact, I understand that they were going to be married.'

Jean-Paul's eyebrows rose expressively. 'Death is sometimes merciful,' he remarked with brutal candour. 'But I have heard nothing of this. She speaks only of Monsieur Dumarais, and how rich she expects to become.'

Marty shot him a startled look. 'As a housekeeper?' she queried. 'I wouldn't have thought it was the best-paid of jobs.'

Jean-Paul shrugged vaguely. 'I think she did not mean that, but she does not speak of these things to me, you understand, only to Madame Benedict.' His voice sank lower, became perceptibly more intimate. '*Alors*, Martine. I shall see you again, *n'est-ce pas*? And at a time when you will have no one else to meet?'

Marty paused. She couldn't say she was startled by the invitation. It had been, she supposed, a foregone conclusion ever since Jean-Paul had joined her at the table, but she wasn't sure how she ought to respond. He was certainly not short on attraction, and if Luc Dumarais' shadow had not fallen across her life, then she would probably have agreed to have a date with him without a second thought.

There was also the additional problem of free time. Nothing positive had been established with Luc about her working hours, and in fact she spent nearly all her time with Bernard. Their days were spent in the open air, and in the evening between dinner and bedtime they usually played chess or backgammon together. While this kind of life was by no means a hardship, it did mean her movements were fairly restricted.

'You do not wish to go out with me?' Jean-Paul was beginning to look a little hurt at her continued silence, and she hastened to reassure him.

'It isn't that. I—I'd like to—really I would. But I don't know when I'll have a day off.'

Jean-Paul looked frankly surprised. 'You work at Solitaire?' he asked, his brows creased.

'Of course.' It was Marty's turn to look surprised. 'What did you think?'

He shrugged rather evasively. 'I did not know. It is not important.'

For a moment Marty was tempted to pursue the matter. It occurred to her that Madame Guisard might have been giving her friends and relations a very different impression of her presence at Solitaire—representing her, perhaps, as some sort of indigent hanger-on. But with an inward sigh, she acknowledged there was little point in getting upset. After all, she had few illusions about the housekeeper's opinion of her. And in two, perhaps three weeks' time she would no longer be here to be disturbed by the older woman's malice.

'Well, I promise you that I do work,' she said eventually. 'And I don't have a great deal of time to myself.'

Jean-Paul laid a persuasive hand on her arm. 'Tomorrow evening there is a disco on the beach. You will go to it with me? You cannot also work in the evening. I will come for you *à neuf heures*.'

Marty nodded slowly. 'Yes,' she said. 'I'll do my best to get away. But you do understand I'll have to mention it to my—my employer.'

'That is easily done.' Jean-Paul's tone was dry, and he

looked past her. 'Here he is now.'

Marty started involuntarily, and twisted round in her chair. Jean-Paul was perfectly correct. Luc Dumarais was walking towards them, his dark face set in thunderous lines. He was holding a sullen-looking Bernard by one arm.

'Oh, no!' Marty's heart sank.

'I think perhaps I go now,' Jean-Paul said tactfully. '*A demain*, Martine *chérie*.'

'Yes.' She barely heard his parting words. Her attention was riveted on the two approaching her. She got to her feet. 'Monsieur?' she faltered. 'What—what's wrong?'

'You dare to ask me that?' His voice was like ice. 'So this is how you regard your responsibilities!'

'I'm sorry,' she said stiffly. 'I wasn't aware that I mustn't bring Bernard into Les Sables. We'll stick to the beach in future if that is what you want.'

'What I want, *mademoiselle*?' His eyes raked her scathingly. 'What I want—what I expect is that wherever you take my son, you exercise some control over his activities. How often do you bring him into town and simply allow him to run wild while you drink with your adolescent admirers?'

'That's most unfair!' Marty stared at him, her heart thumping wildly. 'He just went to buy a few books out of his allowance. What possible harm is there in that?'

His lip curled. 'Is that what he told you, *mademoiselle*? I am afraid you are too gullible. Bernard has been acquiring books, *sans doute*, but he does not spend his allowance on them. In fact he does not spend anything at all. He steals them.'

'What? Oh, I don't believe it!' Frantically, Marty's eyes sought those of Bernard, but he avoided her beseeching glance, and she leaned back against the table feeling a little sick.

'Your beliefs are immaterial, *mademoiselle*. If you had been supervising him as you are paid to do, then all this might have been avoided,' Luc Dumarais said contemptuously. 'Fortunately the proprietor of the bookshop is a friend of mine and he recognised this singularly clumsy thief as my son and telephoned me at Solitaire rather than the gendarmes.'

'I wish it had been the gendarmes,' Bernard said in a low voice. 'I wish I had been arrested and taken to court—and perhaps taken away from you. That is why I did it, *tu sais*. I didn't want his books. I don't want your allowance. I wish to go back to Paris—to my cousin's house. You don't want me, you never did,' he finished breathlessly.

Luc Dumarais' hard eyes considered his young son's flushed face with a bleak expression in their depths.

'*Quand même*,' he said quietly. 'You remain with me, *mon fils*. And you need not betray your natural loathing for me by accepting my money any longer. Your allowance ceases from this moment, *comprends-tu*?'

For a moment Bernard looked oddly stricken, and his lips parted momentarily as if he was about to appeal against this part of his punishment. But in a moment the old sulky look had returned, and his lips were clamped tightly shut again.

Marty stood in silence, her hands tightly clasped in front of her. She was shaking inside with reaction. It had never occurred to her that Bernard was not to be trusted. The first time they had come to Les Sables, he had shown her his money and told her he wanted to choose some books. That time she had gone with him—she had even bought a couple herself, but he had taken so long over his choice and changed his mind so often that she had become bored. So, on the next occasion, she had offered to wait for him at the café while he went to do his browsing. She bit her lip. Was this the first time he had stolen, she wondered bleakly, or had he taken advantage of the gullibility his father had accused her of each time they had visited Les Sables?

Luc Dumarais turned back to her. 'My car is in the square,' he said briefly. 'We will return to Solitaire immediately.'

It was a dreadful journey. She sat in the back of the car beside Bernard who stared resolutely out of the window, refusing to meet her eyes. She felt a total failure, yet only an hour or so before she had been congratulating herself on the progress she was making with Bernard. Her complacency had been short-lived indeed. She wondered what would happen when they got back to the house. Perhaps Luc would dismiss her. In many ways that might be the best thing that could happen, she told herself drearily. If she stayed, what more could she expect but disappointment and heartbreak?

When the car stopped in front of the house, Luc alighted first and opened the rear passenger door. He said something to Bernard in a voice too low for Marty to catch and the boy walked into the house ahead of him, his head bent.

Marty climbed out and stood waiting by the car. Luc turned and looked at her. His face looked strained under its deep tan, and a tiny muscle moved convulsively by his throat.

She had to break the unnerving silence which stretched between them.

'Do you want me to go and pack?' she asked, hating the young, breathless, frightened note in her voice.

'Is that what you wish to do?' he enquired wearily.

She stared down at her sandalled feet. 'You said—that I hadn't been doing my job.'

'Perhaps that is not entirely your fault. I should have realised that the task was beyond you.' His voice was toneless. 'My only excuse is that even I did not recognise the depths of Bernard's determination to be free of me.'

'And is that so impossible?' she said quickly, her heart beginning to beat in swift painful jerks. He was talking to her—not the brief formal phrases of greeting he had used over the past two weeks, but as if she was a person in her own right. 'If he wants so very badly to go and live with his cousins . . .'

'*Non*,' he said forcibly, his tone grim. 'That is something

I will not permit—not now, or ever, no matter what pressure Bernard thinks to bring to bear upon me.' He turned away with an air of finality. 'For now, I have sent him to his room. Consider yourself free for the rest of the day, *mademoiselle*.' The formality had returned, as if he had remembered he was angry with her and why, and had put her at a distance again.

Marty watched him walk away from her and into the house, and remembered she had not asked him if she could have some free time the following night to attend the disco with Jean-Paul. She could hardly run after him now, like a child begging for a treat. Besides, it was hardly a good time to be asking for favours, after what had happened, nor would it help that she had actually been with Jean-Paul while Bernard had been pursuing his embryo career as a shoplifter.

Besides, she thought with sudden rebellion, I am an employee here, not some kind of prisoner. I don't have to ask his permission.

She went into the house and walked up the stairs, intending to go straight to her room, but outside Bernard's door she paused. She could hear no sound from inside. She knocked, but there was no response and she tried the handle, suddenly afraid that he might have run away.

But Bernard was there, lying across his bed. At the sound of the door he lifted himself up on his elbow and stared at her defensively, his face swollen and streaked with tears.

Marty said quietly, 'Bernard—it's silly to go on like this. Your father will never let you go, you know. You're only hurting yourself when you behave like this.'

'Go away,' he said, his voice raw. 'You know nothing. And why should you care anyway?'

'Of course I care.' She took another step into the room.

'You lie,' Bernard said. 'I heard what he said. He pays you to spy on me. You are not a friend, you are a spy. Go away!' He turned his back on her, his young shoulders and arms looking pathetically vulnerable beneath the tee shirt he was wearing. 'Albertine is right,' he said in muffled tones. 'She is my only friend—and you—you are nothing but trouble, as she said.'

Marty went out of the room, closing the door carefully behind her. She was trembling a little as she stood on the gallery. No one wanted her here, she thought, so how in all conscience was it possible for her to remain? She gave a sigh and wearily pushed a strand of chestnut hair back from her forehead. On the other hand how, practically, could she go? She was sure she had come nowhere near earning the salary advance that Luc Dumarais had given her, let alone enough money to enable her to return to England, so it seemed she was still back at square one.

She went into her room and into the small *cabinet*, running cool water over her wrists and applying it to her temples. The rest of the afternoon and evening stretched in front of her. She supposed she could go on the beach, but after two weeks that had begun to pall slightly. Besides, she preferred going there in the mornings before the sun reached its height. She found the sweltering heat of the afternoons a little hard to take. Anyway, the relaxed atmosphere of the beach, surrounded as she would be by hordes of people intent on nothing but enjoying themselves, did not fit in with her own sombre mood. She needed something to do—something to take her mind off her problems, to still the ache in her heart that she did not even want to think about.

With sudden resolve she went downstairs and made her way to Luc's study. Another door closed against her, she thought as she knocked steadily and waited for a reply. But none came and after a moment or two she plucked up her courage and peeped round the door. The room was empty, and it looked as if a hurricane had hit it.

It was the first time she had entered the study and she looked around her with curiosity. It was not a large room, and it was dominated by a massive workmanlike desk on which rested an expensive-looking electric typewriter. The faint humming noise she could hear revealed that the owner of the room had left the power on when he thrust back his chair and went out. Marty walked round the desk and found the button which operated the electricity, pressing it to the 'off' position. There was a half-typed sheet in the carriage, and without surprise she saw that it was set out in screen-play format. Other typed sheets were littered across the top of the desk, many of them with pencilled alterations. There were discarded sheets too, scrunched up into balls, both on the desk and the floor which she kicked as she moved. The wastepaper basket too was overflowing. Marty stared at, making a small impatient noise in her throat. Her years of office training were revolted by the lack of order, even though she knew it was nonsensical to apply the same standards of neatness to a private study belonging to a film director as those of a rather finicky English solicitor. She supposed this must be what they meant when they talked of the creative mind—but did it really need to operate in this type of chaos?

Tentatively she began to straighten some of the muddle of papers around the typewriter, sorting them into strict numerical order. All the dialogue and directions were naturally in French, and as she worked she amused herself by testing her powers of translation. A few of the idioms used escaped her, but she soon caught the drift of what the script was about. It was a powerful story, the central character, a man without a name, opting for solitude and a more or less hermit-like existence after a series of dis-illusionments in human relationships. It was, she decided as she read, a story of moods rather than action, and one of character, the protagonist—she could not call him the hero, because on many occasions he displayed less than heroic qualities—coming through forcefully. A man at odds with himself, she thought, and at odds with twentieth-century society as well. It seemed curiously familiar somehow, and she was quite sorry when her small task was done. She had no idea how many pages made up a finished typescript, but guessed that Luc was nowhere near completion as yet.

He was a fine writer, she thought, as she set the now tidy sheets in a pile beside the typewriter, displaying a sensitivity and an insight into the depths of human nature that he apparently could not apply in his own relationships. Or was it really that the total cruel failure of his marriage, and his son's all-too-natural resentment had taught him too late about the feelings and needs of others? She doubted if he would make the same mistakes in his next marriage—if he married again. A clear image of the beautiful Gisèle Andry rose in her mind, her hand possessively on Luc's arm, her eyes alight with sensuous triumph, and Marty shook her head with a small bitter smile. There could be no doubt that he intended to marry again.

She stood back. The desk was clear now, except for a few packs of typing paper, and two thick notebooks with marbled covers, old-fashioned and obviously well thumbed. A thread of memory stirred in Marty. How funny, she thought. I used to have a notebook like this when I was small. Uncle Jim brought it for me on one of his visits. He wrote in the front of it for me—'Martina Langton—her Book.'

She knew what she was doing was wrong. Luc might very well be angry that she had interfered with his papers. When she had found he was not in his room, she should have simply gone away again. She had no right, no right at all to be in here poking and prying like the spy Bernard had called her.

But there was something she had to know. Stiffly, she reached out and picked up the top book. She opened it and looked down at the page which blurred and swam under her disbelieving gaze. It was Uncle Jim's writing. She would have known it anywhere. She began to read at random, flicking over the pages, realising that what she was reading was partly diary, and partly autobiography written in retrospect.

Eventually she closed the book and sank down into the leather swivel chair that stood behind the desk, letting the book slide on to her lap as she stared in front of her with unseeing eyes.

She knew now where Luc Dumarais had found the plot for his new film, and on whom the central character was based. It was all here—his longing for a settled life, a home, a family, and the fatal flaw in his personality which had defeated him. Uncle Jim, she realised, had been a perfectionist. He demanded the impossible, and allowed his failure to achieve it to sour him, blaming everyone and everything rather than himself.

'What are you doing here?' Her reverie had deafened her to Luc Dumarais' return, but he was there, standing on the other side of the desk, his features distorted by a black scowl.

'When I said the rest of the day was your own, *mademoiselle*,' he said icily, 'that did not give you the freedom to intrude into my *cabinet de travail* and interfere with my private papers.'

'Your papers, *monsieur*?' She held out the notebook. 'Bernard told me that you used people. And he was right, wasn't he? But I thought he was referring to the living. I didn't realise it was possible to go on using people—exploiting them even after they were dead.'

'*Mon dieu!*' He came round the desk and seized her arm, dragging her painfully out of the chair. His eyes blazed into hers. 'You little fool,' he said softly. 'You are fortunate that I do not force every insulting word down your pretty throat. How dare you talk to me of exploitation! I make films. I am in the market for scripts that will make films. Jacques offered me this script not long before he died. It was his life's work, written at long and painful intervals during his life. I knew its quality as I read it, and I agreed to buy it from him—do you know for how much?' He named a sum that made her cry out, and his grip tightened scorchingly. 'I am glad you are impressed.' His voice was

scathing. 'Unfortunately Jacques died before he could bene-
fit from the money—a sad . ending to an unsatisfactory
story.' He took the book from her hands and threw it
down on the desk. 'Or will you say next that I arranged
that too?'

'No.' Shock and his rough handling of her had reduced
her to the verge of tears. 'I didn't know. How could I . . .'

'You admit your ignorance, but still you presume to
judge me.' His eyes raked her mercilessly. He had pulled
her close to him. She could feel his body heat through the
thin dress she was wearing, scorching her at breast, hip and
thigh.

'Let me go—please!' she whispered hoarsely.

'I do not please.' His lips twisted contemptuously. '*Au
contraire*, Martine, you show me a way to punish your
presumption.'

His free hand moved swiftly, tangling in her hair, forcing
her head back.

She said shakily '*No!*' But even that was a mistake because it meant her lips were parted as he kissed her, and she
did not even have that small defence against him. His
mouth was brutal, deliberately hurtful as it explored hers,
bruising its soft contours, and tasting in full the sweetness
no man had ever drunk before.

She couldn't breathe, she couldn't think, the warm male
sensuous smell of him filled her nostrils. In her whole
reeling, shaking world there was no one but this man who
despised her, who only wanted to punish her, whose wild,
violent ravishment of her mouth was prompted by no other
passion but anger and the desire to inflict pain.

And the awful shaming truth was that it didn't matter.
That as long as he went on kissing her, she did not care
what emotion might prompt him. Even his anger was better
than his indifference, she thought incoherently, as her arms
slid upwards to twine round his neck, her fingers convulsively moving in the thick dark hair which grew low on the
nape of his neck.

The hard thrust of his body against hers was a torment akin to madness. She had never known what it was to crave the touch of skin against skin until that moment, and as if he had divined her thought, his hands lifted, tearing open the buttons of his thin shirt, then sliding round to unfasten the zip at the back of her dress. He pushed the thin straps from her shoulders and impelled them downwards, dragging the fragile material of her bodice with them, baring her to the waist. Only then did his mouth leave hers to seek the soft rose-tipped mounds his hands had uncovered.

Her whole body was melting, dissolving into an undreamed-of languor as his lips caressed her swelling nipples. His hands which had been cupping her slender waist moved downwards over the delicate curve of her hips, seeking the smooth warmth of her thighs through the encumbering folds of her skirt. He lifted his head and looked down into her eyes, his own asking a mute question, while his hands moving in slow sensual bewitchment on her body discovered the answer for himself. Then he began to kiss her again, not just her willingly parted lips, but her eyes and her cheeks and the soft tumultuous pulses in her throat and temples.

'*Tu es si belle.*' His tongue traced her ear lobe, and the hollow beneath it, making her press herself shivering against him, the dark hairs on his chest rasping sensuously against her nakedness. '*Mais je veux te voir nue—toute nue, tu comprends?*'

Yes, she understood, and a terrifying shyness came over her. His wish could be easily accomplished, she realised, her mouth dry. There was only her dress which he had half removed already, and the brief panties she wore beneath it, nothing that would hinder his desires for more than a few seconds.

Sensing her hesitation, Luc folded his arms tightly round her, drawing her against him, as if reminding her of the urgency of their mutual arousal.

'*Qu'as-tu, chérie?*' His tongue flickered persuasively

along the passion-swollen curve of her lower lip. '*Tu n'as pas peur de moi?*'

His question made her feel slightly hysterical. Frightened of him! He had to be joking. She was terrified, not just of the way he had proved he could make her feel, but of the uncharted depths which still lay ahead of her. And where was he planning to carry out her initiation? she wondered. Here on the floor of his study, or did he intend to take her up to his bedroom, its shuttered dimness cool and remote from the heat of the day?

She heard herself say in a quiet, stony little voice, 'Don't you think I've been punished enough already?'

His intake of breath was swift and harsh, and then his arms fell away from her and he stepped one short pace backwards. His eyes went over her in one lingering, sensual appraisal, and then with almost insolent ceremony he reached for her, pulling the straps of her dress back into position, and adjusting the flimsy material over her breasts. She burned under his touch, her own gaze fixed wretchedly on the carpet at her feet.

'*Voilà.*' His hands dealt with her zip in one swift upward motion. 'And,' he said with cold and deadly emphasis, 'if you are waiting for me to apologise, *mignonne*, then I warn you that you will wait for ever. Now, get out.'

For a moment she was afraid that her legs would not obey her, and that she would disgrace herself by stumbling without dignity to the door. As she turned away the telephone rang, startling her into a little cry.

Luc's arm brushed hers as he reached for it. She felt the contact achingly, brief as it was, but his face was remote, as if he had forgotten her existence. He lifted the receiver.

'Ah, *c'est toi*, Gisèle. No, *chérie*, you have interrupted nothing. That is,' he added with silken cruelty as Marty reached the door, 'nothing of any importance.'

And the sardonic mockery on his dark face seemed to strike her like a blow, as she wrenched open the heavy door and fled.

CHAPTER EIGHT

MARTY wriggled further into the welcome shade afforded by the striped beach umbrella. She scooped up a handful of sand, and watched with half-closed eyes as the fine grains drifted through her fingers. At noon that day the thermometer had reached a new high, and local people were trying to remember when Les Sables had last enjoyed such a prolonged spell of continuous good weather, and prophesying gloomily that it would soon break in a storm.

The Atlantic breeze was stilled, and the dark blue sea rippled gently on to the sloping beach instead of crashing in its usual breakers. The normal energetic beach games had been abandoned, and nearly everyone had found themselves some sort of shelter, from umbrellas to hastily rigged up awnings. Even the voices and laughter seemed muted, and somewhere near at hand someone was playing a radio, the music it was dispensing providing a softly insidious yawn-inducing rhythm.

Beside her, Marty felt Jean-Paul stir and reach for the sun-tan oil. The first drops on her back felt pleasantly cool, and she moved her shoulders sensuously and he rubbed the oil into her skin. But her pleasure was confined to the soothing qualities of the oil. Jean-Paul's touch meant nothing to her. She supposed she should be grateful that he could apparently accept the fact, and not continually torment her with kisses and caresses that it would be impossible for her to respond to.

She was thankful too that he attributed her reluctance to inexperience and natural English frigidity, and so the truth had never occurred to him. There was clearly not the slightest suspicion in his mind that relations between Luc Dumarais and herself had ever deviated from those of

141

employer and employee. She supposed wryly that neither he nor any of his friends would suspect she was sufficiently attractive or glamorous to arouse the attention of anyone like Dumarais, as they familiarly referred to him among themselves. They spoke of him enviously, commenting freely on his genius as a film-maker as well as his money and his reputation with women, much of which, Marty realised, they had gleaned from scandal magazines. Some of their girl-friends had watched Marty with calculation in their eyes and asked her privately if she could arrange for them to be introduced to Dumarais. She wondered ironically if there would have been quite so many budding film stars among them if Luc had been twenty years older with a bald head and a pot belly. But clearly they regarded her as a potential stepping stone, and in no way a rival, and she was glad of this.

And it was certainly better for Jean-Paul to put down her lukewarm behaviour to him when he attempted to shift their relationship to a more intimate level to timidity and lack of passion than know the truth.

Marty found the truth difficult to face herself. It was as if like some princess in an ancient romance she had lain asleep for years until Luc had awoken her with his kisses. A smile twisted her lips. But even here the analogy broke down, because surely the prince had been tender with his princess. No fairy tale girl would have been made to suffer such a brutal assault on her innocent mouth.

That innocence was gone forever now, she thought, burned away in the fire of Luc's experience. So she had stopped short of the ultimate surrender, had shrunk from the idea of accompanying him to the shuttered shadows of his bedroom for an afternoon of lovemaking, but it made no difference to the way she felt. Ungiven, her body belonged to him just the same, and its aching frustration was his alone to appease.

Jean-Paul's finger feathered its way down her spine, and she moved restively, tacitly rejecting the caress, hearing him sigh a little as he moved away. She was sorry, but there was nothing she could do about the way she felt. She was grateful to Jean-Paul too. She would have been bitterly alone over the last few days without his easy companionship, but gratitude was not an emotion she could transform into the sort of response he wanted, and had probably expected. Besides, she told herself, a virile young man would only take so many rejections, and then she would find that she was the rejected one, watching him walk past with a more accommodating girl, a prospect which roused little more than indifference in her.

She had hardly seen Luc since that afternoon in his study, but she knew that he was working harder than ever. The following day a plump bespectacled girl had appeared at the villa and Marty had learned that Luc had hired her as a temporary secretary only that morning. The move was a calculated one, she knew, designed to show her that she did not even have the subservient position of a typist in his scheme of things. The girl, Sophie, had been bubbling over that first day at the idea of working for Dumarais. It was, she had confided to Marty over a shared lunch, her first job in a private villa, but as the days passed she had become increasingly glum and silent.

Of Bernard, Marty had seen nothing at all. He was confined to his room nearly all the time now, or stayed there through choice. She was not sure which was the truth of the situation.

She had been thankful to be able to escape from the atmosphere of the villa and go with Jean-Paul to the disco, having taken her courage in both hands and asked Madame Guisard for a key to the front door to enable her to get in again afterwards. At first she thought the woman was going to refuse outright, or at least refer her to Luc, but after giving Marty a long thoughtful look, she had eventually produced a key with a grudging air.

Having been rejected by Bernard, and had her secretarial abilities disdained by Luc, Marty had small compunction in accepting Jean-Paul's invitation to spend her time with himself and his friends.

Another girl in a different summer would probably have had little difficulty in falling in love with him, and returned to the English autumn with a few memories to warm the winter days ahead. But not her. She'd had to be fool enough to fall in love with a man whose only need of her, or probably any woman, was an hour's diversion. 'Nothing of importance,' he had said with utter and hurtful dismissiveness. Perhaps for Gisèle Andry the prospect of becoming Madame Dumarais, with its attendant prestige, was compensation enough for marrying a man whose only requirement apparently was a beautiful, willing body. For they were expected to marry. Town gossip said so in the cafés and bars, and there were hopes that the marriage would be celebrated locally and not in Paris, which did not need the attendant publicity.

In the past few days Madame Andry had been a frequent visitor to the villa, her high heels clicking confidently across the hall as she made her way to the study. Presumably interruptions in the day's work from her were welcomed.

Marty wondered if anyone at the Villa was aware or even cared how she spent her days. Had Madame Guisard told Luc that his unwanted house guest now had a key, and came and went as she pleased?

Jean-Paul flicked her cheek with his finger, rousing her from her sombre reverie.

'Chérie, we are going to the cinema tonight. They are showing one of Dumarais' old films. You want that you should come with us?'

For a moment she hesitated. The way she was feeling, anything that served to remind her of Luc was a pain to be avoided. And yet, while she still lived in his house, how could there be any real avoidance?

'Which film is it?' she parried, playing for time.

'Née de la terre.' He paused. 'You would say—earthborn or child of earth. It was one of the films which made his name. Have you never seen it?'

Marty shook her head, and her chestnut hair swung across her cheek, hiding her faint flush.

'I've never seen any of his films,' she said quietly, and Jean-Paul whistled, giving her an amazed look.

'Then come with us and improve your education.' He chuckled. 'Your *patron* would not be too flattered if he knew.'

'He does know,' she said flatly. 'But I'd like to come. Thank you for asking me.'

'It is my pleasure, *chérie*,' he replied, and reached out to stroke her hair back from her face. 'Don't pull away,' he muttered roughly at her instinctive reaction. 'I'm not going to rape you. For one thing, it's too hot. *Mon dieu*, Martine, sometimes I ask myself what is the matter with you! Or is it me? Is there a man—some lover in England perhaps—who can make you respond as a woman should?'

For a moment she stiffened, wondering whether he had guessed her shaming secret, but his mention of England made her relax, even smile a little.

'There's no one.' She turned on to her back and stared out at the blue haze of the horizon, her hand automatically going up to shade her eyes, and hide any trace of wistfulness from his searching gaze. 'I—I'm sorry, Jean-Paul.'

'Don't be sorry.' He shrugged, trying to speak lightly. 'Who knows, *chérie*, my luck may change.'

But not with me, she thought, never with me. Probably nine out of ten girls coming here from England on holiday would have found his rather boyish charm completely irresistible, she knew. It was sad for them both that she should have been the tenth.

Jean-Paul dropped her as usual at the end of the track leading to Solitaire in time for her to change for dinner. Not that there was a great deal of necessity to change these days, as she invariably dined alone.

It was cooler under the shade of the pine trees, and she was grateful for it. Seen through the overhanging branches,

the sky looked an even deeper, purer blue. Dust scuffed up
around her feet as she walked, and she found herself
wondering petulantly if it was never going to rain again.
How ridiculous I am, she thought. This is the sort of
weather people pay hundreds of pounds to enjoy, and all
I'm doing is waiting for it to break. And as she walked up
the track, she realised with a slight flicker of apprehension
that there can be more than one kind of storm.

And part of it seemed to have already broken, because
round the corner of the track came Sophie, Luc's new
secretary, pushing her bicycle, and it was plain that she had
been crying. Her eyes were fixed on the ground and she
was muttering to herself as she came.

Marty paused, and stepped aside. It was clear that Sophie
was too engrossed in her own unhappy thoughts to notice
her, and she didn't wish to be bowled over by a bicycle.

'Sophie,' she asked tentatively, 'is something wrong?'

Sophie glanced up. Her eyes were red but her cheeks
were flushed with something like temper.

'*Je suis un esclave dans cette maison*,' she snapped.
'*Mais c'est fini. Je ne vais pas rester ici. Laissez-moi passer,
s'il vous plaît.*'

'I'm not stopping you,' Marty said rather helplessly.
'But calling yourself a drudge is going rather far. I . . .'

'You!' Sophie glared at her. 'What do you know? When
I work and work, and yet nothing—nothing that I do is
right. And all the time he is angry. *Eh bien*, someone else
can do it now. I am finished—I have had enough!'

She pushed almost rudely past Marty and walked on,
trundling her bicycle and grumbling under her breath.
Marty stood for a moment, watching her go, then she
turned and went on up to the villa.

She went in the front door, just in time to see Madame
Guisard on her way to the dining room carrying the large
tureen of soup, so she dropped her handbag down on the
carved chest that stood against one wall, and followed her
into the dining room.

Tonight, it seemed, she would not be dining alone. Luc was already sitting at the table when she went in and Madame Andry was with him. For a moment, Marty hesitated, but it was clear they had both seen her, and she would merely make herself ridiculous if she now beat a retreat like a scared rabbit. So she walked to the table and took her place with a murmured apology for her lateness.

Luc acknowledged her presence with a curt nod, while Madame Andry stared right through her. It occurred to Marty, giving her a furtive look under lashes, that Gisèle Andry was not in a very good temper. She smiled and talked, and used her elegant hands, displaying the fine rings she wore, but there was a tell-tale spot of colour in each cheek, and a slight sense of strain about the conversation she was hell-bent on maintaining.

Marty tried not to look at Luc at all. She had not expected to see him there, although she supposed Sophie's belated and tempestuous departure should have given her a clue, but she was conscious of his presence through the entire meal, even though he never spoke to her or glanced in her direction as far as she was aware.

She was thankful when the cheese board arrived and she was able to excuse herself.

'*Un moment, mademoiselle, s'il vous plaît.*' Luc's voice detained her as she reached the door. She looked round and saw that he had risen and was coming after her. 'A word with you in private, if you please,' he said silkily. He led her away across the hall to the *salon*, but not before she had caught a glimpse of Gisèle Andry's face, sullen with displeasure.

He closed the *salon* door behind them and looked at her in silence for a moment. She found his gaze unnerving but was determined not to let him see it. Every nerve-ending in her body, every pulse was reminding her of the last time they had been alone together, and its disastrous aftermath. Why did he want to see her now? Was it to tell her that it was time she got out of his house, out of his life for ever?

'I have had to dismiss that girl from Les Sables who was working for me,' he began abruptly. 'She was useless—emotional and without intelligence. But there is still a considerable amount of work to do on the script. You claim to have had secretarial experience, and your other duties are apparently curtailed at the moment, so——' He made a slight gesture with his hand.

Marty stared at him disbelievingly. She said, 'You want me to work for you?'

'That is the last thing I want.' The harshness in his voice stung her. 'But it seems I have little choice. And you told me once you wished to earn your fare home. *Eh bien ...*'

Marty was very pale as she faced him. She said gently, 'You're quite right, *monsieur*. That's what I did say, and I meant it. What time do you wish me to begin in the morning?'

'I usually begin around eight o'clock. However, I don't necessarily expect such an early start from you.'

Marty lifted her chin. 'I'll be there.' She paused. 'After all, the earlier I make a start, the sooner the job will be finished, and I can leave.'

'To return—home?'

The mockery in his voice was undisguised, as if he knew quite well the pit of loneliness that awaited her anywhere but here. What did he expect her to do, she wondered half-hysterically, fling herself at his feet and plead with him to let her stay on any terms?

She was proud of the note of faint surprise in her voice as she said, 'Naturally, *monsieur*. Where else would you expect me to go? Now if you'll excuse me, I must get ready. I'm going out.'

'Are you still seeing that student?'

The question halted her in her tracks. She had not been expecting it, and she turned to face him, her eyebrows lifting.

'As a matter of fact, yes. Is—is it any concern of yours?' What on earth was she hoping for? she wondered despairingly. That he would say something—anything that would show he cared about her.

'Hardly,' he shrugged a shoulder. 'But I feel some sense of responsibility for you, and it would not enhance your future prospects in England if you were to return there *enceinte*.'

Marty flushed. 'There is no likelihood of that,' she said in a low voice.

'*Non?*' He lifted a cynical eyebrow. 'Is this admirer of yours such a paragon of virtue?'

Her breathing quickened slightly. 'I don't have to answer your questions,' she said at last. 'I can't understand why you're asking them. Unless you're worried that someone else might succeed where you failed,' she added with a flash of reckless temper.

His eyes narrowed. 'You have reverted to that bad habit of flattering yourself, *mignonne*.' His voice bit at her. 'Hasn't it occurred to you that I might not have been trying very hard?'

It was cruel, but then he'd intended to be. What was he trying to make her understand? That his lovemaking had been a whim, since regretted? A brief unimportant incident, easily brushed aside, and certainly not to be repeated? She supposed that for her own sake she ought to feel relief, but all she was capable of was desolation.

As she reached the door, she heard him say, 'Martine', on a note of anger, but she slipped through the door as if she had not heard, closing it quietly behind her, and he did not come after her.

She was hardly in the mood for a cinema visit, but she showered quickly and changed into a brief denim skirt, and a cool striped shirt with long sleeves. She looked round for her shoulder bag and realised she had left it downstairs on the chest in the hall.

As she went downstairs, her heart sank. Gisèle Andry was standing at the foot of the stairs, tapping her foot impatiently. Her mouth was tight and set, and she no longer looked the sophisticated, glamorous companion of a well-known film director. She looked merely bad-tempered.

'I want a word with you, *mademoiselle*.' Her voice was harsh as if she was having a struggle to control it.

Marty suppressed a sigh as she walked past the older woman and retrieved her bag.

'I'm at your service, *madame*,' she returned with more courtesy than she actually felt. 'But I'm just on my way out.'

'I shall not take long,' Gisèle Andry said flatly. 'I just wanted to give you this.' She was wearing a hip-length matching jacket over her oatmeal dress, and from the pocket she produced a roll of banknotes and held them out towards Marty, who could see at a glance that there was more than five hundred francs in the roll. 'Well, take it,' she went on. 'If it is not enough for the purpose then you must let me know. I am not *au fait* with these things, but I can visit my bank tomorrow and ...'

'I'm sorry,' Marty interrupted, bewildered. She made no attempt to take the money which Madame Andry was practically thrusting into her hand. In fact, she took a step backwards and put both hands behind her back as a child might do. 'I don't understand. Enough for what purpose—and why should you give me money anyway?'

The older woman's laugh was almost strident. 'Don't play the *innocente* with me, *mademoiselle*. You want to go back to England, but are prevented from doing so because of money. I also want you to go and am prepared to help. It is quite simple.'

'Is it?' Marty said slowly. She could feel anger beginning to boil up inside her, but was determined to control it. 'Everyone seems to want me to go.'

'Then why are you so insensitive as to remain?' Madame Andry asked bluntly. 'Aren't you ashamed to accept Luc's charity?'

'I'll hardly be doing that.' Marty faced her defiantly. 'I shall be typing his script for him as from tomorrow, and

the last girl he hired walked out in tears this afternoon,
describing him as a slavedriver. He doesn't sound particularly charitable.'

Madame Andry laughed again, but there was no amusement in the sound. 'And you of course would welcome the
opportunity to become Luc's slave. That is most evident.
Petite imbécile, do you think I care if he chooses to amuse
himself with you?'

Marty said quite gently, 'You seem to care, *madame*,
very much. But you really have nothing to worry about. I
do not intend to become Monsieur Dumarais' mistress.
Your place in his life is perfectly safe.'

Gisèle Andry's face was mantled with an unbecoming
flush. She said '*Salaude!*' and her hand shot out and caught
Marty's cheek in a stinging slap.

For a moment Marty stood in silence and looked at her.
Temper had made the lovely face suddenly ugly, and there
was fear mixed with triumph in Gisèle's eyes. She wanted
to put up a hand and nurse her cheek which was hurting,
but she knew the other woman would see it as a sign of
weakness, a request for sympathy, so instead she forced her
suddenly dry lips to smile before she turned and went out
into the evening air.

Jean-Paul was waiting for her at the gate, and he leaned
forward at her approach to open the door for her. His eyes
searched her face as she got into the battered passenger
seat.

'*Qu'as-tu, Martine?* You are very pale, and there is a
mark here.' He touched her cheek lightly, and she could not
stop herself from wincing. He noticed at once. 'What is it?'
He looked more closely. 'Someone has hit you, *non*? Who
was it? Not Dumarais, surely. Was it Bernard?'

She shook her head. 'It was neither of them. I'd rather
not talk about it, Jean-Paul. I had a quarrel with someone
and came off worst. To tell the truth, I'm a little ashamed
about the whole thing.'

'But you're shaking.' He watched her with frank concern.

'Shall we forget the cinema? Would you prefer to have a drink—or perhaps drive somewhere?'

'Oh, no!' She hoped her rejection did not sound too hasty, but she wanted to avoid a situation where she and Jean-Paul would be alone together in case his protective air became too intimate. 'I—I want to see the film. I need something to take my mind off what has happened.' She stole a glance at him and saw that he looked unconvinced. 'Really, I'm all right. It was just a shock, that's all.'

He shrugged and started the engine of the car. 'It was a little more than that, I think. You will have a bruise.'

Marty was very quiet as they drove into Les Sables and parked the car in the square. There was no cinema as such, but films were shown during the season in a small hall, just off the square, which was also used for dances. During the drive and the subsequent walk to the hall, all Marty could think of was Gisèle Andry's face, twisted with dislike, the angry wounding words. She supposed she should really pity her. Madame Andry had claimed she did not care how Luc amused himself, but it was plainly not true. Marty thought drearily that if she was planning on making their relationship a permanent one, her life would be much easier if it were true.

All Bernard's accusations against his father were true, it seemed. Luc Dumarais was just a womaniser. Probably he could not help himself. And while he confined his activities to women who knew the score, everything was probably fine.

But Marty knew nothing except that from almost the first moment she had registered his attraction, and that all her subsequent struggles against it had been in vain. Even before he had kissed or touched her, she had wanted to be in his arms, had known what his caress would do to her.

And yet to him it meant nothing. A brief flare-up of passion which for once had stopped short of the final consummation, and was now placed firmly in the past, as far as he was concerned, demonstrating with finality just how little his own emotions had been involved. Or had he guessed her own feelings, and merely backed away, because however he might choose to amuse himself, his real commitment was to Gisèle Andry?

Marty suppressed a sigh. Perhaps she should have taken Madame Andry's offer at its face value, and accepted the money. Probably if she had liked the older woman better, or thought that her motives were prompted by a genuine concern for a young girl wholly out of her depth, she might have done so. As it was, it seemed that Gisèle Andry was prepared to pay well over the odds to get rid of her, and she found herself wondering why.

Her thoughts seemed to be going round in circles, and it was almost a relief to find herself in the stuffy crowded little hall, waiting in the half-darkness for the film to start. Her cheek still throbbed slightly, and she lifted her fingers gingerly to touch it and discover there was a faint swelling.

After a few advertisements, greeted with whistles and catcalls from the predominantly young audience, the film began, and with a sense of shock Marty realised that the leading role was being played by Victorine Cajoux, Luc's late wife. She supposed she should have known it would be so. After all, Jean-Paul had claimed it was one of the films which had made his name, and Bernard had told her how closely their early careers had been linked. The provocative but controlled sexuality that Marty had divined from the still photographs was even more evident on the screen. It was an odd, disturbing story, and she was soon totally absorbed in it.

Victorine Cajoux played the part of a young girl living with her aunt and uncle and young cousins in the depths of the country—a girl convinced that she had magical powers, and who practised strange rites in a little grove near her uncle's house. The film traced her small triumphs—the prevention of her cousin's marriage to a young man she herself wanted, the dismissal of a housekeeper who had become aware what was going on, and the gradual disintegra-

tion of her personality, as she drew more and more people
into the sphere of her imaginary powers. But as the film
proceeded to its brutal and shocking climax, it became apparent that many of the questions it raised were not going
to be answered. Was the girl really a witch or had she
merely blundered on some formula which enabled her to
raise the powers of destruction? Or had the seeds of destruction always been there within her?

As she followed Jean-Paul out of the hall into the warmth
of the night air, Marty could not be sure. But she could
acknowledge the power of Victorine Cajoux's performance
—those knowing eyes in the innocent loveliness of the face,
like a child with an unpleasant secret. It had made her feel
uncomfortable, yet she didn't really know why. It was difficult to believe that it was Luc's wife and Bernard's mother
whom she was watching.

She joined in little of the heated discussion of the film
which followed in a nearby café. For one thing, she
couldn't follow all the debate, and for another, she was
immersed in her own thoughts. She wondered when the
film had been made. It must, she was certain, have been
before Bernard was born. She knew that it had only been
acting, and that films were never made with their scenes
in strict chronological order, but surely Victorine Cajoux,
with a small son of her own, would have jibbed at the
climax where she had to murder her uncle's youngest boy.
And how could Luc, who had directed her in the part, have
borne to see her performing such an action?

She shook her head, telling herself fiercely that she was a
fool. Actresses did what they were told, and directors made
films from scripts that other people had written. Except that
Luc—sometimes—made films from scripts of his own devising—didn't he? She thought of the notebooks with
Uncle Jim's manuscript, and the pages of typing which
she would help him complete in the morning.

Jean-Paul laid a hand over hers. 'What are you thinking,
chérie?'

'About the film,' she said, and gave a little involuntary shiver.

'You did not admire it?'

'Yes,' she said slowly. 'I couldn't help doing that. But I didn't—like it. I don't know why he made it.'

Jean-Paul shrugged. 'He made it because he is in the business of making films.' He paused, then said in a different voice, 'She was very beautiful, *non*?'

'Very,' Marty agreed levelly. There could be no argument about it. All through the film, Victorine Cajoux's physical beauty had been insisted on—almost lingered over, and in most of the woodland sequences she had been naked. Marty knew that nudity in films and on television was commonplace these days, but not quite so much, she thought, when that film was made. She wondered if Luc had ever felt jealous when he saw other men—the film crew perhaps—watching Victorine, desiring that perfect body. It was impossible to imagine it swollen and shapeless in pregnancy.

From the other side of the table, a girl called Stephanie that Marty had met only once broke into their conversation.

'*C'est incroyable, n'est-ce pas?* Even then there was no sign.'

Marty was jolted as if Stephanie had spoken her own thoughts aloud. She said, 'You mean—the baby?'

Stephanie stared at her. She was a pretty girl, with waist-length hair, studying something very erudite, as far as Marty could remember, at the Sorbonne.

She said impatiently, '*Mais non*. You work there, do you not? Then you of all people must know ... Unless he does not speak of it.'

'Speak of what?' Marty persisted. 'I don't know what you're talking about.'

A silence had fallen round the table. Some of the group, Jean-Paul included, were looking as baffled as Marty felt.

Stephanie's eyes were filled with amazement. She made a little gesture. 'Then you do not know ... I am sorry. I should have said nothing. I thought everyone knew. They always kept it from the papers, but word spreads ...' She shrugged.

'Word of what, Stephanie?' someone urged.

She shrugged again, flinging an almost apologetic glance at Marty. 'Victorine Cajoux was a drug addict.'

There was a silence, then Jean-Paul said sharply, *C'est impossible, ça.*

'No, it is true,' Stephanie said. 'An uncle of mine is a doctor in Paris, and she attended one of his clinics. I would not have known, but when she died he spoke of the case to my parents, and I overheard. He said she had made experiments with drugs since she was very young—that someone in her own family had introduced her to them, but that she had always believed that she could be cured whenever she wished. That she would always be stronger than the drugs. But the time came when that was no longer true.'

Marty said, 'Oh, God!' The air in the café had become suddenly suffocating. Someone in her family, she thought. The family to which Bernard wanted to be sent. Was there any wonder that Luc was so bitterly opposed? Yet, knowing what he did, why had he allowed Bernard to stay with his mother during all those vulnerable, impressionable years?

There was a babble of talk round the table and she was able to hide behind it, thankful that no one was looking at her, requiring a reaction or a comment. The news had been a small sensation, revealing quite clearly how successful the concealment had been up to that point. But now?

Les Sables was a small place, and gossip could spread like wildfire, Marty knew. Sooner or later, it would reach back to the house at Solitaire—to Bernard, whose stubborn belief in the woman who had been his mother was the foundation of his small world. It was, after all, all that he had.

She felt sick. Could this be why Luc Dumarais had chosen to bury himself so far out of the mainstream—so that there was time for any talk after his wife's death to flare up and die down again for ever?

If so, then his plan had failed, and she knew she had to get back to the villa and warn him of what had happened. The prospect made her flinch inwardly. No doubt by this time Gisèle Andry would have given him her own edited version of the scene which had occurred between them, and she could envisage Luc's wrath only too clearly. She had had no right—no right at all to say what she did, and to add to that she now had to be the bearer of unwelcome tidings.

She moved abruptly, pushing back her chair and stood up. Jean-Paul rose with her. '*Qu'est-ce qui se passe?* What is the matter Martine? Are you ill? You are so pale.'

She seized gratefully on the excuse he had given her. 'A—a slight headache, that's all. It was so hot in the cinema. I think I'd like to go home.'

She shook hands with everyone in the group, forcing a smile, trying to pretend she had not seen the long, considering totally undeceived look that Stephanie had given her, and the fact that before she had reached the café door, the other girl had bent forward to engage her nearest companions in a low-voiced conversation that Marty was convinced concerned her.

But there was no time to worry about what was being said. She had to get back to Solitaire and tell Luc that his secret was a secret no longer.

Jean-Paul was all concern as he took her to the car. On their arrival back at the villa he offered to escort her up to the house, but she declined with more haste than politeness and slid out of the passenger seat. He was clearly disappointed that he was not even to be granted his usual goodnight embrace, but he drove off with a brief wave. No doubt he would go back to the café in Les Sables, Marty thought as she went up the drive, and no doubt it would not be many minutes before Stephanie and her companions were giving him their interpretations of her silence and pallor, allied to her hurried departure.

She almost ran up the drive. Gisèle Andry's car was not there, which was a relief, and the house was in darkness on the ground floor. She reached the front door and fumbled inside her bag for her key, but it wasn't there. She paused, puzzled, for a moment, then rummaged through her belongings again before unceremoniously dumping them out on to the doorstep. The key was not among them, and her mind noted that something else was missing too, although she did not give it a great deal of attention. The most pressing matter was that the key seemed to have vanished, and without it she could not get into the house.

She groaned aloud, then stood back a little way, studying the first floor windows. There was a glimmer of light coming from Bernard's room at least, and after only a moment's hesitation she reached down and collected a handful of small pebbles. She hurled them upwards with all her strength and heard them clatter against his shutter. Then she waited. If he was awake, and he must be or otherwise his light would be off, then he must have heard her. He could so easily come down and let her in. She had not the slightest wish to rouse the entire household. It must be much later than she had realised if everyone at Solitaire had gone to bed, and her interview with Luc would have to be postponed to the morning.

There was still no sound from the window above her. She craned her neck, staring upwards.

'Bernard!' she called softly, and gave a low whistle, but there was no response.

She was beginning to get cold. A slight breeze had sprung up, and its chill was penetrating her thin shirt. She risked a louder call. 'Bernard!'

There was no way he could have failed to hear that, but the only response was silence. With a feeling of slight desperation, Marty went back to the front door and tried it, just in case someone had left it open for her, but it was a forlorn hope. Then she searched her shoulder bag again, digging into every corner and every pocket in case the key might have got jammed somewhere, but that too was a waste of time. The key had vanished, and yet she had replaced it in her bag after using it last time. She knew she had. She could remember doing so. Could it have fallen out while she was on the beach? It was a possibility, and an annoying one because it implied carelessness on her part, and Luc would not be pleased to know that there was a key to his house lying round somewhere for anyone to find.

Marty sighed and pushed her hair back from her face with a little irritable gesture. Was there any point, she wondered, in going down to the beach and searching for the key? After all, she knew almost the exact spot where she had spent the afternoon. Jean-Paul and his friends used it every day. But she had no torch, and it was very dark now, with only a slip of a moon to guide her. Yet she had to do something. She could hardly spend all night in the open.

The breeze came again, and she shivered, rubbing her hands protectively up and down her arms. There was nothing to be gained simply by standing still and freezing. She began to walk round the house, pausing to try ground floor windows, and even the double doors that led on to the patio. But the Villa Solitaire seemed impregnable to attack.

At the back of the house, she paused, staring upwards again. She had spotted an open window, its shutters only pulled casually together. She tried and failed to work out which room it was, but the important thing was it was a means of access because there was a thick creeper of some kind growing up the wall almost to roof height, unlike the front of the house which was totally bare. She tugged at the creeper tentatively, but it resisted her efforts, and the stems and branches seemed rope-thick. It might just support her weight.

She swallowed. It seemed it was either a scramble, gambling on the chance of a fall and a broken limb, or a night spent in the open, and she felt she would rather risk the broken limb. She took hold of a branch of the creeper, tested it to make sure it would bear her weight, then began to climb, moving very slowly and resting frequently. The creeper in fact presented few difficulties. The stems were thick and tough, and provided plenty of footholds. Marty was soon level with the window. She reached out and grasped the underside of the nearest shutter, drawing it back against the wall. She eased herself along the branch she was standing on until she could reach the windowsill. It felt reassuringly solid under her fingers and she breathed a short sigh of relief. All she had to do now was pull herself across and up, and she would be in the room.

And then the light in the room came on, dazzling her so that she cried out and slipped, and heard the branch crack under her foot. She thought, 'I'm going to fall.' And as the full horror of the thought crystallised in her mind, hands came down, gripping her, sliding under her armpits to drag her across the windowsill. She landed on her knees on the softness of a carpet and looked up into the dark, furious face of Luc Dumarais.

She looked round the room incredulously. The bed was rumpled, its covers thrown back, and Luc was in a dressing gown, its sash loosely knotted round his waist, his feet and legs bare.

Marty said quite inadequately, 'Oh, dear,' and her hand came up to cover her mouth like a guilty child's.

CHAPTER NINE

THERE was a moment or two of electric silence, then Luc said grimly, 'I am waiting for your explanation, *mademoiselle*.'

Marty said feebly, 'I'm sorry. I—I didn't realise this was your room.'

He swore violently under his breath, and hauled her to her feet. 'Little *imbécile*!' He shook her, his hands hurting her arms. 'It doesn't matter whose room it was. Do you not realise you might have been killed?'

'It was quite safe,' she said quickly. 'All but the last bit—and then you helped ...' Her voice died away when she encountered the blaze of anger in his eyes.

'And if I had not been here to help?' he asked bitingly. 'What then?'

Marty threw back her head, finding courage from somewhere. 'I would have been all right,' she returned with dignity. 'It was only you putting the light on which startled me, and made me slip.'

'So it is now my fault.' His lips were tightly compressed, and the dark brows drawn together in a chilling frown. 'And it is also my fault, I suppose, that you decide to enter my house in this foolhardy manner. Does the conventional means of entrance no longer appeal to you?'

She said, 'I couldn't get in. I've lost my key. I—I didn't want to wake everyone—and then I saw this window. But I didn't know it was your room.'

He smiled thinly. 'Or wild horses would not have prevailed on you to climb up. Is that what you were going to say?'

'I wasn't going to say anything,' she said wearily, and to her shame and fury felt tears filling her eyes. It was tired-

161

ness, she knew, and the combined shock of first hearing
about Victorine Cajoux and then her enforced climb, but it
was a sign of weakness which she didn't want to display
in front of Luc.

Luc saw the tears at once and turned away with a
muttered, '*Dieu!*'

'I'm sorry.' She scrubbed furiously at her eyes. 'I didn't
mean to wake you or anyone. I'll go.'

She headed blindly to the door, but somehow he was in
the way blocking her path.

'Not so fast.' His hand went under her chin, lifting her
face to his relentless gaze. 'So you did hurt yourself.' His
fingers brushed the bruise on her cheekbone, and she
winced slightly. He swore softly. 'But that's impossible,' he
went on half to himself. 'The bruise would not have come
out so soon.' His eyes narrowed. 'Who did this thing to
you? Your student friend?'

'Oh, no,' she denied swiftly. 'It—it was an accident.' His
hand still rested against her cheek. Marty swallowed. She
had an overwhelming urge to turn her head, to press her
lips against the fingers that touched her, to place them on
her breast. Her heart said, Be angry, be anything, but hold
me, love me, and she was afraid for him to look into her
eyes.

He said with a kind of scornful derision, 'An accident.
And how did this accident occur?'

She shook her head, not trusting her voice.

'You would prefer not to tell me?' His voice hardened.
'*Eh bien, ça ne fait rien.*' His hand fell to his side, and she
was left desolate.

'There's nothing to tell,' she said lamely.

'Don't lie to me, Martine. Did you really imagine that
you could stay out half the night, bruise your face, and
then climb into my bedroom without being asked a single
question? Do you imagine I have no sense of responsibilty
where you are concerned?'

That stung. 'You don't have to feel responsible,' she

cried. 'You—you're not my uncle.'

He smiled unpleasantly. 'No, I am not, am I, *mignonne*. Perhaps that is something of which I should remind us both.'

She said on a little shaken note, 'Luc—no!' But it was too late. His arms had already reached for her, his hand hooking almost insolently around the nape of her neck, pulling her towards him.

He said mockingly 'Why say "no", *chérie*, when you mean "yes"? If you meant "no" you would have played this dangerous escapade of yours at another window.'

He gathered her close against him, and she realised for the first time that he was naked under the thin dressing gown. His lips brushed hers in the merest breath of a caress, then sought the long vulnerable line of her throat. Marty gave a little breathless sob and tried to pull away, but his arms were ruthless in their strength, bending her backwards so that she was forced to cling to him to maintain her precarious grip on her balance.

She whispered, 'Luc—I—you must listen to me.'

'I am listening to your heart beating, *mignonne*.' His teeth teased the lobe of her ear. 'That tells me all I need to know.'

'You don't understand,' she insisted desperately. The slow tantalising movement of his mouth against her flesh was destroying her will, her reason.

'Don't I?' There was sudden cyncism in the dark eyes as they looked down into hers. 'Mine is the realm of make-believe as well, *chérie*. I make films—or had you forgotten? And your next line is "Be gentle with me." *Bien, c'est entendu.*' He smiled without mirth. 'Was that perhaps where your student lover made his mistake? Did he want to play rough?'

'*No!*' His words hurt as if everyone were a whiplash laid to her skin. 'I did see Jean-Paul tonight, but it isn't as you think. We went to the cinema in Les Sables. It was one of your films. Your—your wife was in it.'

She had his full attention at last. The arms which held her were suddenly tense.

'She was in a number of my films,' he said at last harshly.

'I know. Afterwards we were talking about it—a crowd of us. There was a girl there called Stephanie. Her uncle was a doctor. He—knew your wife, knew why she died.'

'And now you know too. That is what you are trying to say, *n'est-ce pas*? Well, it is said. Do you imagine I still mourn for her? Is that why you are here tonight—to comfort me in my sorrow?' He flung her away almost contemptuously. 'Keep your pity, *ma mie*. I don't need it in my life, and particularly in my bed. Victorine died for me many years ago—long before the drugs took her.'

'But she didn't die for Bernard,' she said in a low voice. 'You let him live with her—feed him with whatever lies she chose to tell about you. What are you going to do now, Luc? Now that the truth has caught up with you. Keep him locked up here at Solitaire so that he'll never hear it? You really do inhabit a realm of makebelieve if that's what you think.'

He turned away. 'He loves her,' he said expressionlessly. 'His belief in her is all that he has. I can't destroy that too. And I know the sort of thing she has told him. It was to punish me, you understand, for the failure of her career —which she herself had destroyed. Already there were rumours. The filth she was taking had affected her temperament. She was late—she could not learn her lines—there were hysterical scenes—she fought with other actors. The list went on and on. And that quality that she had—that look of depraved innocence—that too was gone. Only the depravity remained.'

'She told Bernard that it was because she'd lost her figure in giving birth to him,' Marty whispered. 'She told him that you taunted her about it—that you'd never wanted her to have a child.'

'That at least is true,' he said tautly. 'Oh, not as she told it. Of course I'd wanted a child—when we were first married—when I still thought that our lives together had a chance. Later, when I found out about her drug-taking, I thanked God she had refused to have a baby—it can affect an unborn child. I could not risk that.'

'But she—did have Bernard.'

'Yes.' He passed a hand wearily across his eyes. 'We had not been sleeping together. She knew that I intended to leave her. One night there had been a party and I came back to the apartment very late. I had been drinking. She —came to my room.' He sent her a hard look. 'You have seen her—I don't have to explain what happened. When she told me she was *enceinte*, I thought at first she was lying. I nearly went mad when I discovered it was true. She thought the child would keep me with her. As long as she had me, she believed there would continue to be films for her. By some miracle, Bernard was born unharmed. I wanted to take him with me when I left, but she would not allow that. She pleaded with me—said she had given up the drugs. That the baby had given her a purpose in life— something to live for even if our marriage was over. She said if I took the baby, she would kill herself. At the time I believed her. I did not realise that it was inevitable.'

The stiff, almost disjointed account ceased. He moved over to the window and stood staring out into the darkness.

'So few people knew,' he said half to himself. 'Friends— colleagues may have had their suspicions, but they said nothing. Even the gutter press did not get hold of the story. I thought if I could get Bernard away—right away—then there might be a chance, but I've failed. Victorine did her work too well, and now the whispering has started again, even here.'

Marty said, 'Luc—I'm sorry,' and he turned on her so violently that she flinched.

'*Diable*, haven't I said that I do not want your pity? You've said what you came to say, now go.'

'I don't pity you!' she flared. 'If there's anyone I feel sorry for in this whole stinking mess, it's Bernard—torn this way and that between the pair of you. It's time you had a little compassion of your own—for your son!'

The tears were spilling over again uncontrollably, and with a little gasp she turned and fled for the door.

'Martine.' Luc reached her as she was fumbling for the handle, and swung her round to face him. 'God in heaven,' he groaned, 'what am I to do with you?' He pulled her to him while she wept, her wet face pressed against the bare skin of his chest, until at last she rested quietly in his arms. At last he set her a little way from him and looked down into her face, his own cool and unsmiling.

'It's time you were in bed,' he said quietly. 'No, your own bed, *mignonne*, not mine. I think you've had all the emotion you can handle for one night, and while at some future time I shall probably be happy to hold you in my arms while you sleep, that is not what I want at this moment. So I shall take you back to your own room and wish you *bonne nuit*.'

She wanted to protest, to fling herself back into his arms and tell him she did not want to be alone for what was left of the night, but she restrained herself. She was quiet until they reached her bedroom door, which he opened for her and stood waiting for her to go into the dark room beyond. Suddenly he was a stranger again, dark and remote, a prey to his thoughts, and she could not bear it. She moved to him and put her hand on his arm.

'Goodnight, Luc,' she said gently, and raised her face for his kiss.

For a moment he hesitated, then he bent his head and touched his mouth gently to hers. It was as if he had lit a flame within her. Almost involuntarily, her body arched hungrily against his, her fingers digging into his muscular shoulders pulling him closer as his kiss deepened, hardened at her response, and his hands made a slow pilgrimage of pleasure from her waist to the ardent thrust of her breasts. She clung to him without reserve, returning kiss for kiss, glorying in his touch, and the warm scent of his skin.

And then it was over. Luc was wrenching her away from him, dragging her arms from round his neck.

She gave a little cry. 'Luc—don't leave me . . .'

'In the name of God, Martine.' His voice was ragged. 'I need a woman in my arms, not a child needing comfort!' He turned and went down the gallery and out of sight. In the distance she heard his door slam, a sound that seemed to echo close at hand. Then, slowly and wearily, she went into her room and closed the door behind her.

She was pale and heavy-eyed as she made her way downstairs the following morning. She was late. It was already past the hour when Luc had said he normally started work, so she went straight to the study and knocked on the door.

His '*Entrez*' sounded curt and impatient as if he had already started work and resented being disturbed. As Marty entered, he barely glanced up.

'I've put the typewriter in the dining room,' he said briefly. 'You can work undistracted there. Perhaps you would save any queries until the afternoon. I want to work in peace this morning and I am going to be out at lunchtime.'

She stared at him, open-mouthed. 'But—I thought I'd be working in here—as Sophie did.'

'And I have said I prefer you to work in the dining room.' His dark brows drew together in a swift frown, and he glanced at his watch. 'Perhaps you would like to make a start. There is a great deal to get through.'

She bit her lip. She was at more than arm's length again, it seemed, and it hurt. She had been fool enough to hope that after last night they would be closer to an understanding. When he had talked to her about Victorine, she had been happy to think that he felt he could confide in her. When he had spoken of her sleeping in his arms, it had seemed as if he visualised a future in which she had a part. Yet today, it was as if a door had been slammed in her face.

She was a tiresome necessity to be shunted off out of his way.

She turned on her heel and went off to the dining room. It was all ready for her—the typewriter already plugged in, the pages for re-typing in a neat pile, and boxes of clean paper to hand. She sat down at the table with a little sigh. This was why she had agreed to stay all those weeks ago. She was simply doing the job she had been hired for, so there was no reason at all to feel slighted. And when Luc was in this sort of mood, she could see why Sophie had fled from the house in tears and temper.

She had never tried to type in a foreign language before, and found it more difficult than she had anticipated. Her usual speed deserted her, and her accuracy, but how far this was due to the unfamiliarity of the work she was handling and how far to her state of emotional turmoil she would have found it hard to say.

By mid-morning, however, she felt she was winning at last, and she was quite glad when the door opened and the dour figure of Madame Guisard appeared with a tray of coffee. For a moment, Marty hoped that Luc might join her. Then she saw the single cup on the tray and resigned herself to a solitary break.

'Will Mademoiselle have lunch here or in her room?' Madame Guisard enquired. Her eyes went over the small pile of typescript at Marty's elbow, and she permitted herself a brief, smug smile.

'It doesn't matter,' Marty lifted the pot and poured herself some coffee. 'Monsieur will be out.'

'That is true,' the housekeeper nodded. 'He has arranged to lunch with Madame Andry. He was telephoning her a moment ago when I took him his coffee.'

Marty sat very still for a minute when the door had closed behind Madame Guisard. Her hand lifted almost of its own accord and touched the livid mark on her cheekbone. A small bitter smile touched her lips. So now she knew the reason for Luc's change of attitude this morning.

Daylight, it seemed, had brought a return to sanity and realisation of where his real commitment lay.

She pushed the heavy typewriter away from her and put her head down on her folded arms on the table. She wanted to cry, but she had shed enough tears in this house. She had no doubt that Luc found her sufficiently attractive to indulge her with a brief *affaire* before she returned to England, but that wasn't what she wanted. She knew now with the utmost clarity that she wanted to belong to him body and soul, that she loved him and all she craved was his love in return. A night—even a few nights of passion could not assuage the deep ache of longing within her. She didn't want a brief illicit romance. She wanted to be Luc's wife, to have the right to sleep with him, and to spend her days with him too. She wanted to give him a child—one that would be carried and borne without shadows or bitterness. She wanted the earth with the moon and the stars thrown in.

She sat up slowly, feeling cold and sick inside, then dragged the typewriter back into position and began to type as if her life depended on it. Nothing halted her, not even the unmistakable sound of Luc's departure for his rendezvous with Gisèle Andry about an hour later. A little sob rose in her throat and was rigorously controlled.

The door behind her opened a little while later, and she went on working, expecting it to be Madame Guisard with her lunch. But to her amazement, Bernard's voice said *'Bonjour, Tina.'*

Her fingers stilled on the keys and she swung round to face him. 'Bernard—you're quite a stranger!'

He nodded. 'You permit that I call you Tina?'

She shrugged. 'You may if you wish. That's what Uncle Jim used to call me—after my mother. She was always Tina to him. It's a long time since anyone's called me that. You—startled me.'

'Yes,' he said, and there was an odd almost gleeful note in his voice. 'I thought that I had done so.'

Marty stared at him. She said, 'It's rather funny, isn't it? You haven't wanted to be my friend for days now, and now suddenly you do again. Why?'

He shrugged evasively. 'It is lonely, always to be by myself. I bear you no malice, you understand. You obeyed Papa's orders. It is your duty.' He gave her an insinuating look. 'And you are glad to obey them, are you not, Tina? You would gladly do anything that he tells you. You want to please him so that another night he will not leave you at your door, but go into your room with you and . . .'

'Stop it!' Marty gazed at him in horror. She was remembering things now. That odd echo of Luc's door closing. 'You were there last night—watching us. How dare you!'

He grimaced. 'I could not sleep,' he said offhandedly. 'Something woke me. I came to my door, and Papa was there with you. Were you sorry, Tina, when he went back to his own room, and left you there all alone?'

Marty's cheeks flamed. 'Get out,' she said coldly and clearly. 'And don't come near me again.'

Bernard's eyes filled with unexpected tears. He came forward and put a hand on her arm. 'I am sorry, Martine. Forgive me. I did not mean to say these things.'

'Didn't you?' Marty asked rather grimly. 'How odd, because it seemed to me you'd come down here for the express purpose of saying them. However, let it pass.'

'It is just that I am sorry for you,' Bernard explained. 'I told you, did I not, what Papa was like, and yet, all the same, you permit him to make a fool of you.' He sighed. 'It is very sad. I think you will be very unhappy, and I do not want that.'

Marty sent him a wry glance. 'Thank you. But you really don't have to bother about me.' She picked up the page she was working on and studied it, trying to get back into the flow of what she was doing, but a thought was nagging at the back of her mind.

'You say something woke you last night,' she said. 'But when I got back you were still awake. Your light was on, and I tried to attract your attention.'

'I heard nothing.' Bernard's eyes were wide and innocent. 'Why should you do such a thing, I ask myself?'

Marty turned back and stared at him for a long moment. 'I should be interested to know what reply "yourself" returns,' she said pleasantly. 'Shall I tell you what I think? I think you were still awake because you were waiting for me to come home and discover that the door key was missing from my bag. I think you were sitting up in your room enjoying the idea of me throwing stones at your window and prowling around down below trying to get in, and you were just waiting for me to start hammering on the door and waking the whole house up. Only it didn't happen, and after a while curiosity got the better of you and you started to go downstairs to see what had happened to me, only to see me on the gallery with your father. That's what I think,' she added with a faint snap. 'I remember now, I left my bag downstairs before dinner. There was plenty of time for you to see it and decide to take the key out of it. You wanted me to come back late and get into a row, didn't you?'

She didn't need an answer in words. Bernard was looking both sullen and guilty at the same time.

'It was a joke,' he insisted defensively. 'I did not mean that you should stay outside the whole night. I would have let you in—after a time.'

'Many thanks for small mercies,' Marty said drily. 'Perhaps you'd like to go and get the key now. And I've remembered something else. I missed another thing from my bag last night while I was hunting for that blasted key—Uncle Jim's letter. That's how you knew he called me Tina, wasn't it? Because you took it and read it.'

She had expected more guilty sulks, but to her surprise Bernard came a step closer and his small face grew almost eager.

'Martine, you will be glad that I read that letter, because I can prove to you now that Papa only wants to make a fool of you. This work that you do for him, it is from

Jacques' book, *non*? Papa was to have paid Jacques a great deal of money for this when the film is made, but because *le pauvre Jacques* dies he does not get a single franc. So who should get that money instead, Tina?'

Marty felt a long cold shiver pass over her. She said, 'Bernard, what happened was between Jacques and your father. It's none of our business.'

'But it is your business. Jacques did not make a will, but before he died, he wrote on a paper that you should have all the money that was due to him. I saw the paper. It is in Papa's study. He knows the money for the film is to go to Tina, and yet he says nothing of it to you. Instead he makes you work, and then he makes love to you a little, so that you will think he is wonderful, and when the summer is over you will go back to England and smile when you think of the great Dumarais—and never know how he has cheated you.' His voice grew suddenly shrill and he banged on the table with his fist. 'I told you, Martine. I told you that he would use you. He is making a fool of you.'

Marty had her hands to her ears. 'Stop it, Bernard! I don't believe you—I won't . . .'

'Then why are you working in here?' he demanded. 'The other girl, the fat Sophie, she worked in the study with Papa because it did not matter what papers she did or did not see. There was nothing to be kept hidden from her.' He tugged at her arm. '*Venez*, Martine. You will see that what I say is right.'

She felt quite numb as she rose from her chair, and followed Bernard. Money, she thought. There had been thousands of francs involved because Luc had told her so, and all the time he had known that Uncle Jim had intended her to have that money. How he must have been laughing at her! Her heart cried out with anguish at the very idea, but they were in the study now and Bernard was opening the drawers in the big desk, finally producing an orange folder with an air of triumph. '*Voilà!*'

The folder was full of papers, most of them, she saw, to

do with the projected film and its costings and budget. Papers covered in typing and figures. Official papers. That was all.

She said, 'There's nothing there, Bernard, and we have no right to be in here.'

'But I have found it,' he said, and got up from his knees, holding a smaller sheet of paper. It was Uncle Jim's hand-writing. She would have known it anywhere.

It said, 'Any money owing to me when the film is made is to be for Tina,' and it was signed. The writing straggled a little, as if it had used up the writer's strength, and tears came into her eyes. He hadn't wanted her to know that he was ill, or that his dream house had been sold to someone else, but he had thought of her at the end, and planned that the unexpected fortune which had come to him too late should be hers.

'I told you that there was a paper,' Bernard said at her side.

'Yes,' she said very quietly. 'You told me.'

'He would have kept you here,' the small voice went on. 'He would have made you work for him. But you will go now, won't you, Martine? And when you are in England you will make your lawyers write to Papa, and claim all the money so that you can be happy.'

'No,' she said, still in that quiet voice, 'I—I shan't do that, Bernard. But you're right about one thing. I can't stay here, not now. I must leave at once.'

She supposed she ought to thank him. He looked shrunken suddenly and rather lost, but she could not find any grateful words. How could you thank someone for taking every hope, every bright dream you had ever had and smashing it?

'Will you leave a note for Papa?' His eyes were fixed on her face.

'No.' She shook her head. 'I'll just leave him this.' And she unclenched her fingers and let Uncle Jim's last wish drift down to the carpet. Then she went to the door.

*

Marty kicked off her sandals with a small sigh of relief and stretched herself out on the narrow bed. Through the partly opened window she could hear the faint hum of traffic, and the distant cry of gulls brought on the breeze from the sea. Occasionally there were the sounds of footsteps and voices and laughter from the street several floors below, but even these were muted as they reached Marty in her small room under the eaves.

It was indeed very small. After space had been found for the *armoire* with its hanging cupboard and large drawers, the bed and a chair, there was barely room for Marty herself, and she sometimes wondered ruefully how Madeleine, Madame's daughter who had been built on more redoubtable lines and who had been the room's previous occupant, had made out.

Marty flexed her tired muscles and chided herself for ingratitude. She had this room as shelter, and she had a job, and that was altogether more than she had dared hope for when she had fled so precipitately from Solitaire only a week before. Was it really only a week? Sometimes it seemed like a lifetime. A lifetime of loneliness and regret.

She had had no very clear idea where she was bound for when she boarded the mini-bus which circulated between the town of Les Sables and the neighbouring beaches and small communities which had sprung up around them. But once she had arrived in Les Sables, it had seemed the most sensible course to seek out Jean-Paul and ask his assistance.

He had just come off his shift at the bakery, and had intended to make his way back to his room for some sleep, but that idea was abandoned when he saw the anguished urgency in Marty's pale face. He leapt of course to the obvious conclusion—that Luc had tried to make love to Marty against her will, and had panicked her into flight, and she let him go on thinking so because it was easier than embarking on the genuine explanation. Besides, being a practical Frenchman, he would never understand, she knew, why she had left the house without the money that had been intended for her, and she would never be able to convince him in a thousand years that it was not the money that was important, but the fact that Luc had deceived her and cynically used her, and in so doing had betrayed the memory of a dead friend.

That was what hurt. What little she knew of the relationship between Luc Dumarais and Uncle Jim seemed to have been based on mutual trust. Luc had bought his house and enabled him to go on living there, and had cared for him until his death. And Uncle Jim had trusted him with his manuscript.

Marty sighed and pressed a clenched fist against her quivering lips. But with Uncle Jim dead, Luc must have felt that was the end of his obligation. He could have had no idea that a claimant would ever appear, and when she did —why, she was easily fobbed off with an offer of a job and a roof over her head for a few weeks. It must have amused him to see how easily he could transfer the sense of obligation to her.

And it must have amused him even more to see what other senses he could carelessly awaken. The little girl would have other memories to take back to England with her. She supposed she could only be thankful he did not know how well he had succeeded. She had never actually said the fatal words 'I love you' and betrayed herself completely.

In the end, she had begged Jean-Paul to take her to La Rochelle. If Luc went in search for her, she reasoned, he would look in the direction of the Channel ports, not to the south. Not that she believed that he would search. The realisation that she knew the truth might cost his conscience a few pangs, but his overmastering reaction would probably be one of relief that she had left without making trouble. And he would probably never even ask himself why.

Jean-Paul had argued with her, suggesting that he should take her to stay with his family in Brittany, but she had resisted this. Acceptance of his offer would be bound to lead to greater intimacy between them, and a sense of debt on her part which she didn't want.

La Rochelle was a city, and there would be work there. She would find something to do to earn her sufficient money to get her home again. They were already on their way when she remembered the restaurant where Luc had taken her, and Madame Verner's smiling offer to teach her to cook. She would go there. They might know of someone who needed a kitchen hand or even a waitress. Jean-Paul was not happy about her decision, but he was clearly relieved to know that he would not be depositing her in a city of total strangers.

He had asked questions as they drove, naturally, and she had answered at first at random, and then more cautiously as she realised their tenor. It was clear that Jean-Paul had been putting two and two together about her open reluctance to become emotionally involved with himself, and her relationship with Luc Dumarais, and she sensed that he had guessed altogether more than she wanted him to about her feelings towards Luc. It was obviously a blow to Jean-Paul to realise he had probably wasted several weeks in pursuit of a girl who had already lost her heart elsewhere, but she hoped it was only his vanity which had suffered.

By the end of the journey he was beginning to probe with frank curiosity into her motives for running away. If she was attracted to Dumarais, and he to her, then everything marched. Why then had she run away? The whole matter was clearly beyond Jean-Paul's comprehension, and her halting explanations only confused him further. He could see no necessity to complicate the pleasure such an *affaire* could have brought her with scruples about love.

Even now, the memory of his bewilderment brought a reluctant smile to Marty's lips. He had shaken her hand warmly at parting, and given her a brotherly kiss on the cheek, and then driven off with a wave, promising that he would be in touch. Marty doubted it.

She had presented herself rather reluctantly at the restaurant, but to her surprise both Monsieur and Madame Verner recognised her instantly and welcomed her in, although the place was closed for the afternoon between the aftermath of the midday meal and the start of preparations for dinner. In spite of this, a bowl of soup appeared miraculously, accompanied by a thick slice of paté with bread and a dish of fresh green salad.

Marty had forgone her lunch at Solitaire in her haste to get away, and until she picked up her spoon and started to eat her soup, she had not realised quite how hungry she was. The Verners let her eat, and then Monsieur Verner made a discreet withdrawal to the kitchen to allow his wife to question Marty.

Marty told her simply that she needed work, and hoped that Madame could recommend her somewhere even though it was late in the season. Madame declared that she could remain with them. Had she not said to her husband only that day that they needed help in the restaurant? They were neither of them as young as they had been. And there was a room for her which could be prepared instantly, the room of her own daughter, now married and living in Angers.

Marty had protested vehemently, but had been overruled. A weekly wage had been fixed upon, and she had been absorbed into the Verner ménage. And the name of Luc Dumarais was never mentioned at all—or at least never in Marty's hearing.

She had to work for her money and she was glad of it. By the end of the day, it was bliss to be able to retire to the little room at the top of the house too tired to think even.

It was during the long afternoon when Madame commanded her upstairs inexorably for a rest that sleep was elusive and memories returned to re-open old wounds. She found herself re-living it all—every kiss Luc had given her, every caress, every word.

Sometimes she found herself in the depths of a wild dream that he was here beside her, his mouth crushing hers, his hard body pinning her to the mattress, and awoke crying his name, tears wet on her face.

She kept telling herself it would be easier once she was back in England, away from all these constant reminders of Luc. During the first couple of days she had been on edge every time a solitary man entered the restaurant, but now at last she had begun to relax. Perhaps Luc was not a frequent visitor to La Rochelle after all, and if he did come, he might not always patronise the same restaurant.

It was cold comfort she was offering herself, but it was all that she had. To know that she would go away from here and never see him again was agony, but it was a necessary agony. And when his film was made it would probably come to London and she would go and see it, and perhaps there would be an interview on television in one of the film programmes. She had seen, without really noticing, that there had been such interviews with foreign directors in the past—sometimes whole programmes devoted to their careers. If she could bear to watch.

She got up listlessly and collected a fresh dress and a handful of clean underwear before making her way down a floor to where Monsieur and Madame Verner had their living accommodation. She went into the shower cabinet, and stripped and showered, washing her hair for good measure. It was getting long, she thought critically, viewing herself in the small mirror as she towelled it dry into a gleaming chestnut cap which framed her face. Maybe if she had it cut it would make her face less thin-looking—although it would do nothing to improve the shadows beneath her eyes.

By the time she had rinsed through the garments she had discarded and hung them on the line in the little courtyard at the back of the restaurant, it was time to help with the preparations for dinner. She was permitted to help with the vegetables, though she was denied any part in the actual cooking as yet. And Madame encouraged her to watch all the various processes, telling her it was the best way to learn.

The customers began arriving early that evening, and soon the trickle had become a rush, with Marty hurrying between the kitchen and the dining room, her arms laden with dishes.

She had just deposited a platter of luscious *langoustines* before one party of appreciative diners, when Monsieur Verner touched her arm hurriedly. 'The table in the window, Martine,' he directed before hurrying on with the bottle of wine someone had ordered.

She picked up the leather folder of menu-cards and started towards the table he had indicated, and then she saw him. He was alone and very much at his ease, watching her unconscious progress towards him with an enigmatic look. She had forgotten, if that were possible, just how attractive he was. She could see some of the women at neighbouring tables stealing looks of frank appraisal at him, then exchanging shrugs and smiles with each other. And someone had recognised him, because on her right she heard a whispered 'Dumarais' and a ripple of interest.

She stopped, saw him begin to rise, and turned and fled back to the kitchen, pushing past Monsieur Verner as she went. Madame turned from the stove, eyebrows raised, spoon in hand as Marty ran in.

Marty looked at her across the kitchen. Her voice was broken as she said, 'Madame, he's here—I can't . . .'

Then she turned and dashed for the stairs that led to the Verners' living quarters and the sanctuary of her room. She slammed the door shut and leaned against it, wishing with all her heart that there was a key in the old-fashioned lock that she could turn.

Not that he would follow her, she told herself as she forced her trembling legs to take her over to the bed. She had made it more than clear by her precipitate retreat that she didn't want to see him, and her behaviour would have created quite enough of a sensation without him starting in hot pursuit. It had probably been as much of a shock for him as it had been for her, she reasoned, and by this time he had undoubtedly left. And she ignored the tiny voice which whispered that he hadn't seemed shocked at all.

Besides, although he might be a friend of the Verners, he was still a customer and it was unlikely that they would give him *carte blanche* to wander through their home at will in search of her. She was safe here for the moment.

And then as if to give the lie to the thought's reassurance, she heard footsteps coming up the wooden stairs which led to her room. She shrank back against the wall as if the action would make her invisible, telling herself desperately that it wasn't Luc—far more likely it was Monsieur Verner come to tell her off for making a scene in his restaurant. And she waited for the knock on the door.

But no one knocked. Instead the door opened and Luc walked in, supremely elegant in the palest of grey trousers, topped by a frilled white shirt and a black expensively cut jacket. In one hand he was carrying a bottle and two glasses. In the other he held a large key.

He closed the door behind him and gave her a long considering look.

'Clothilde sends you this,' he remarked, and held up the key. 'She does not favour the locking of bedrooms as a rule, but she feels there comes a time in the life of every *jeune fille* when such a course of action may be necessary, *alors . . .*'

He tossed the key on to the bed beside her.

'Get out of my room,' Marty said between her teeth.

He smiled mockingly. 'So that you can use your key? I think not. We have things to say to each other, Martine, and I have no wish to be forced to speak to you through a door. So you will sit chastely on your little bed, and I will sit here on this chair and we will drink a glass of Philippe's best wine together and talk.'

'Oh, God!' Marty pressed her hands to her burning face. 'You mean—you got him to give you that wine and then you followed me up here? What will everyone be thinking?'

His smile widened. 'I would not have thought that was in very much doubt.' He poured some wine into each glass and handed one of them to her. 'Take it,' he ordered. 'You look as if you need it. You're thinner, you foolish child, and infinitely paler. What has caused that? Are Clothilde and Philippe unkind to you?'

'No,' she denied indignantly. 'They've been everything that is kind.'

'Unlike myself?' he supplied as she hesitated. 'But you see I did not realise it was kindness you wanted from me, Martine.' He waited for a moment, but she did not say anything, so he continued. 'You looked surprised to see me downstairs, *mignonne*, yet you must have known that I would find you.'

'I see no reason why you should have done,' she said in a low voice.

'*Non?* Yet you must be aware that I owe you some money.'

So that was all it was. A belated attack of conscience.

'Well, you needn't have bothered,' she said tautly. 'I don't want your beastly money. I never did.'

'But you worked for it, *chérie*,' he said quite gently, and tossed a small bundle of notes over to her. 'The remains of your salary.' He smiled again. 'Or did you think I meant something else?' Then, his voice roughening suddenly, '*Dieu*, Martine, why did you run away? Why didn't you stay and ask me for an explanation?'

'I didn't want an explanation,' she said in a low voice. She took a sip of the wine in her glass, feeling it caress the back of her taut throat like velvet. 'After all, there was nothing legally binding on you to give me Uncle Jim's money. It was just a piece of paper. There weren't even any witnesses.'

'You seem to be under a misconception, *ma chère*,' he said harshly. 'You talk as if I had known all about this— piece of paper. Yet the first time I saw it was on the floor of my study when I arrived back at Solitaire that day.' He drank some of his wine. 'I wasn't expected back quite so early, or I imagine it would have been removed.'

She said hoarsely, 'Removed by whom?'

He shrugged. 'By Bernard, *naturellement*, or perhaps by your rival claimant.'

'My rival?'

'Albertine Guisard—who could not wait to assure me that she was the Tina mentioned by your uncle. She told me often enough that as his promised wife she was entitled to some of the proceeds from the film, and that she would prove her claim at the right time. Once you were out of the way, I suppose she thought it was safe.'

Marty set the glass down on the floor beside the bed. 'I don't understand.'

'It's quite simple. Jacques wrote that note when he was very ill. He intended it for me, but I was not there, so he gave it to Bernard to give to me. He liked the boy. There was an affinity between them as there sometimes is between the young and the old. Only Bernard did not give it to me. Jacques died, *tu comprends*, and he was upset. In the meantime Albertine came to him. She knew what Jacques had done. She may even have brought him the paper and the pen, and she told Bernard that she and Jacques had been engaged to be married, and she was the Tina mentioned in the note.' He sighed. 'Unlikely, perhaps, that such a dragon of a woman would have allowed Jacques or anyone else to call her Tina, but she convinced Bernard. But he didn't give her the paper at once. He would give it to her when the time was right, he said, if she would help him achieve his heart's desire to get away from me and return to Paris and his mother's family. And it's fair to say that she did help him. Her complaints about him were endless—even to accusations of him having stolen food from the larder. Neither of them were to know that no ploy would be enough for me to do as they wished.'

He looked across at Marty and smiled suddenly, a smile

that made her mouth go dry and her heart leap in her
breast in a sweet, shuddering excitement.

'And then you came, *ma petite*, and *la pauvre* Albertine
realised at once that here was the real Tina.'

'So that was why she always behaved as if she hated me,'
Marty said incredulously.

'She certainly did not trouble to conceal her dislike. Her
only hope was that you would leave before the truth became
known. So once again she and Bernard joined in league.
They hoped you would be dismissed after the episode of
the books. After all, you were responsible for Bernard and
he had taken advantage of you. I would have been justified
in concluding you were a failure as a companion for him,
and getting rid of you. Only they had reckoned without one
thing, *ma chère*.'

Her voice was barely above a whisper. 'What was that?'

'That I had fallen in love with you, *mon coeur*, and that I
would not let you go.'

She said, 'Oh,' and snatched up the wine glass again,
taking a hasty sip that nearly choked her.

'Then they decided to take away the key you had been
given, presumably so that you would disgrace yourself by
coming in at dawn after a rendezvous with your lover. But
it was then Bernard discovered your letter—the one he himself had posted to bring you to France—and his curiosity
got the better of him. He read it, and saw you addressed as
Tina, and realised that Madame Guisard had been deceiv-
ing him. He was coming to find you that night—I think to
tell you everything—when he opened his door to find us
together, and he knew then that at last he had the perfect
weapon to use against me. I wanted you, so you should be
taken from me. But what he did not realise then that he
was also using the same weapon against himself. He had not
realised in fact how fond he was of you himself. It was only
when you had gone that Bernard discovered what it was to
be really alone. Also in hurting me, he had hurt you badly,
he knew, and that too he had not bargained for.'

'And he told you all this?'

'Not at once. At first, I thought it was Albertine's doing alone. She had left the house by that time—she went as soon as I told her that I had seen Jacques' letter to you when he called you Tina. She realised at once her little game was over.' He paused. 'In a way I was glad that you were not there to hear the names her foul tongue called you.'

'Of course, I remember now!' Marty said numbly. 'Jean-Paul said something once about Madame Guisard expecting to be very rich. But I didn't know ...'

'Neither of us knew,' he interrupted. 'I could never quite believe her story that she and Jacques had been in love, but I could not disprove it either. Certainly she had worked for him ever since he came to Les Sables, and stranger things have happened.'

Marty looked down into the ruby depths of the wine and said, 'Yes,' very quietly.

'Once she had gone, Bernard began to tell me the truth. Perhaps even then he thought that this might be what was needed for me to send him away.' He sighed. 'So in return, I also told him part of the truth.'

'About his mother?'

'No—but about her family, and my very good reasons for wishing to keep him apart from them. It was not merely the drugs, you understand. There were—other things that I will not distress you with. I think I frightened him. He has been very subdued ever since, but when I told him today that I was going to bring you home, he was pleased. He said he had missed you.'

Marty cleared her throat. 'That—that's nice,' she managed. 'But how did you know where I was?'

'Philippe telephoned to me. He said "Luc, we have your little one safe, but I think she is breaking her heart."' He paused. 'You don't answer, and you don't look at me, Martine. Was he wrong, then? Is it your student you are grieving for, and not me?'

She said with difficulty, 'You know quite well. But, Luc, it's no good. You were sorry for me, and then you felt responsible for me, and now you think I've had a raw deal from—from Bernard and Madame Guisard. That's all it is.'

'Look at me, *mignonne*,' he said gently. 'Tell me it's only pity that you see in my eyes. I love you, *mon amour*. I didn't expect it. God knows I didn't even want it to happen. But my house is empty without you, and so is my life.'

Her mouth trembled. 'Empty? With—Gisèle Andry around to—keep you company? The day I left, you were with her.'

'Didn't you hear me say that I returned to Solitaire earlier than expected?' he said. 'Yes, I went to see her—but to tell her that everything was over between us, because I was going to ask you to be my wife. She wasn't—pleased. It seems she had decided to marry me herself.' His lips twisted slightly. 'I cannot imagine what had prompted that decision. We had been close, but our relationship had begun to cool. I was frankly amazed when she followed me here and took a house for the summer.'

'But she was still your mistress.' Marty forced herself to say it.

He leaned his head back against the wall and looked at her. 'What do you want me to say, *ma mie*? That we were just good friends—that it was an *affaire* of the spirit only? It wasn't. *Au contraire*. But that is all there was. I enjoyed taking her to bed, as would any man. But I never wanted her to live with me, to sit at my table, to share my thoughts, to have my child. And that is how I want you, Martine. If it isn't enough—if you can't forgive me for the past ...' He broke off and drank the rest of the wine in his glass.

She said shakily, 'But I don't belong to your world.'

'What world? I am my world. If you belong to me, then you belong to my world. But perhaps it's none of these things. Perhaps you just don't love me enough. The good God knows I don't pretend to be easy to live with, and there's the problem of Bernard. And you're hardly more than a child yourself.'

'But you treat me as a child. And at times I thought you hated me—sending me to work in the dining room, when even Sophie was allowed to work in your study.'

'Oh, Sophie,' he said ruefully. '*Pauvre petite*, how I made her suffer—just because she wasn't you, *mon coeur*. Yet I knew my self-control would crack if I had you working with me, close to me each day. I had to get that script done, and I reasoned that my best method was to keep you at a safe distance—in working hours at least. My plans for that evening were very different.'

She glanced at him shyly. 'What were they, Luc?'

A soundless laugh shook him. 'Dinner *à deux*, *mon ange*, and then bed. What else?' He shook his head. 'And then I returned to the villa, and they told me you'd left without a word of explanation. *Dieu*, I never want to live through another moment like that. It's as well for Bernard that he delayed his confession.'

'What did you do?'

'I went back to Les Sables and found your—boy-friend.' He smiled grimly. 'He told me you were hitch-hiking to Calais. I spent two wasted days checking out what he had said, and our next encounter was even less friendly than the first. But he still wouldn't tell me where you'd gone— just some story that you were in love with me, but didn't want to sleep with me. That was another bad moment,' he added reflectively.

Her cheeks were on fire. She said quickly, 'I had to tell him something, Luc. I—I couldn't tell him the truth.'

'Why couldn't you?' he said slowly. 'You had been led to believe that I was a liar and a cheat. Why couldn't you tell him?'

'Because it would have hurt me,' she whispered. 'Because I love you.'

The glass she was holding was knocked to the floor, spilling its contents across the strip of faded carpet as he came to her, pulling her roughly into his arms.

'*Dieu*, I thought you would never say it,' he muttered, then his mouth was on hers as it had been in her dream, but with an undreamed-of tenderness mingled with his passion, and her lips parted beneath his in joyous response as her arms crept up round his neck to draw him closer still.

Some time later, he said lazily, 'So we'll be married as soon as it can be arranged?'

'Oh, yes,' she said with a little sigh. She stirred slightly in his arms. 'I suppose we should go downstairs and tell Monsieur and Madame Verner. I don't know what they must be thinking.'

'I do,' he said, and there was a hint of laughter in his voice. 'But go downstairs if you must, *ma belle*. You'll cause a sensation.'

'Oh!' Marty crimsoned as she looked down at herself. 'I—I didn't realise.' She gave a little shaken, half-embarrassed laugh. 'This is all so new to me, Luc. I was so miserable and now I'm so happy. I can't believe it's true, that it's really happening.'

He drew her to him again, his hands and mouth very gentle. 'I could make it real for you, *mon amour*. If you belonged to me completely, then you would have to believe it. But you must choose. I can wait for our wedding night, if that is what you want.'

Suddenly she was shy again, but she made herself look up into his face and meet the intent gaze of his dark eyes. The beginnings of a smile curved her mouth, and she put up a hand to touch his face.

'I—I don't want to wait any longer,' she murmured. 'Oh, Luc, I love you so.'

He kissed her again, a kiss which left her trembling and breathless, yet at the same time oddly eager, then he swung himself off the bed and stood up.

He bent and picked up the key which had fallen to the floor beside the bed.

'Clothilde was right,' he said looking at it thoughtfully.

'There comes a time in the life of a *jeune fille* when this becomes an essential. Your time is now, my sweet one.'

And moving without haste, he walked across the room and locked the door.

Titles available this month in the Mills & Boon ROMANCE Series

RETURN TO DEVIL'S VIEW *by Rosemary Carter*
Jana could only succeed in her search for some vital information by working as secretary to the enigmatic Clint Dubois — and it was clear that Clint suspected her motives . . .

THE MAN ON THE PEAK *by Katrina Britt*
The last thing Suzanne had wanted or expected when she went to Hong Kong for a holiday was to run into her ex-husband Raoul . . .

TOGETHER AGAIN *by Flora Kidd*
Ellen and Dermid Craig had separated, but now circumstances had brought Ellen back to confront Dermid again. Was this her chance to rebuild her marriage, or was it too late?

A ROSE FROM LUCIFER *by Anne Hampson*
Colette had always loved the imposing Greek Luke Marlis, but only now was he showing that he was interested in her. Interested — but not, it seemed, enough to want to marry her . . .

THE JUDAS TRAP *by Anne Mather*
When Sara Fortune fell in love with Michael Tregower, and he with her, all could have ended happily. Had it not been for the secret that Sara dared not tell him . . .

THE TEMPESTUOUS FLAME *by Carole Mortimer*
Caroline had no intention of marrying Greg Fortnum, whom she didn't even know apart from his dubious reputation — so she escaped to Cumbria where she met the mysterious André . . .

WITH THIS RING *by Mary Wibberley*
Siana had no memory of who she really was. But what were Matthew Craven's motives when he appeared and announced that he was going to help her find herself again?

SOLITAIRE *by Sara Craven*
The sooner Marty got away from Luc Dumarais the better, for Luc was right out of her league, and to let him become important to her would mean nothing but disaster . . .

SWEET COMPULSION *by Victoria Woolf*
Marcy Campion was convinced that she was right not to let Randal Saxton develop her plot of land — if only she could be equally convinced about her true feelings for Randal!

SHADOW OF THE PAST *by Robyn Donald*
Morag would have enjoyed going back to Wharuaroa, where she had been happy as a teenager, if it hadn't meant coming into constant contact with Thorpe Cunningham.

Mills & Boon Romances
— all that's pleasurable in Romantic Reading!

Available September 1979

Forthcoming Mills & Boon Romances

CHATEAU IN THE PALMS by *Anne Hampson*
Philippe de Chameral could have made Jane happy — but he did not know that she was a married woman . . .

SAVAGE POSSESSION by *Margaret Pargeter*
Melissa had been too used to having her own way to allow Ryan Trevelyan to dominate her — but she soon had to change her tune!

ONE MORE RIVER TO CROSS by *Essie Summers*
Rebecca was as different from her flighty cousin Becky as chalk from cheese, but the girls' identical appearance was to get Rebecca into a difficult situation with the bossy Darroch . . .

LURE OF EAGLES by *Anne Mather*
An unknown cousin had inherited the family business, and Domine found herself agreeing to the masterful Luis Aguilar's suggestion that she accompany him to South America to meet the girl.

MIDNIGHT SUN'S MAGIC by *Betty Neels*
Could Annis ever make Jake see that she had married him for love, and not on the rebound?

LOVE IS A FRENZY by *Charlotte Lamb*
Seventeen-year-old Nicky Hammond's devotion was touching, but Rachel couldn't possibly return it. Yet how could she convince his disapproving father Mark that she wasn't cradle-snatching — or worse?

THIS SIDE OF PARADISE by *Kay Thorpe*
Gina's so-called friend was after a man with money, so Gina couldn't really blame Ryan Barras when he got entirely the wrong idea about her . . .

A LAND CALLED DESERET by *Janet Dailey*
LaRaine had always been able to twist men round her finger but, as luck would have it, she fell in love with Travis McCrea — who had no time for her at all!

TANGLED SHADOWS by *Flora Kidd*
Kathryn could hardly refuse to return to her husband when she learned from his family that he had lost his memory in an accident — but would he remember what had destroyed the marriage in the first place?

THE PASSIONATE WINTER by *Carole Mortimer*
Piers Sinclair was her boy-friend's father: older, more sophisticated, far more experienced than she was. And so of course Leigh fell in love with him . . .

— all that's pleasurable in Romantic Reading!
Available October 1979

Forthcoming Classic Romances

A GIRL ALONE
by Lilian Peake

Sparks had flown between Lorraine Ferrers and Alan Darby from the moment they met — and it was all Lorraine's fault, for not trying to conceal her prejudice against him. Then, unwillingly, she found herself falling in love with him — but hadn't she left it a little late?

JAKE HOWARD'S WIFE
by Anne Mather

Jake Howard was immensely attractive, immensely rich, immensely successful. His wife Helen was beautiful, intelligent, well bred. A perfect couple, in fact, and a perfect marriage, everyone said. But everyone was wrong . . .

A QUESTION OF MARRIAGE
by Rachel Lindsay

Beth was brokenhearted when Danny Harding let her down, and vowed that it would be a long time before she fell in love again. But fall in love again she did — with Danny's cousin Dean, a very different type of man indeed, and one who really loved her. Or did he? Surely fate wouldn't be so cruel as to strike Beth again in the same way?

WHISPERING PALMS
by Rosalind Brett

The discovery of mineral deposits on her African farm came just at the right time for Lesley, but besides prosperity, it brought a scheming sister determined to get most of the spoils herself and to marry the most eligible bachelor in Central Africa.

Mills & Boon Classic Romances

— all that's best in Romantic Reading

Available October 1979